Leslie Charteris

Leslie Charteris was born in Singapore on 12 May 1907   1919 he moved to England with his mother and l   ier and attended Rossall School in Lancashire befo   oving on to Cambridge University. His studies there   ame to a halt when a publisher accepted his first nove   His third book, entitled *Meet – The Tiger!*, was writt   1 when he was twenty years old and published in 1928   It introduced the world to Simon Templar, a.k.a. the S   int.

H   continued to write about the Saint up until 1983, whe   he last book, *Salvage for the Saint*, was published by H   lder & Stoughton. The books, which have been tran   ted into over twenty languages, have sold over 40 milli   copies around the world. They've inspired fiftee   feature films, three TV series, ten radio series and   comic strip that was written by Charteris and syndi   ted around the world for over a decade.

Le   e Charteris enjoyed travelling, but settled for long   eriods in Hollywood, Florida, and finally in Surre   England. In 1992 he was awarded the Cartier Diam   d Dagger in recognition of a lifetime of achieve-ment.   Ie died the following year.

LESLIE CHARTERIS

The Saint in Europe

Series Editor: Ian Dickerson

MULHOLLAND
BOOKS

HODDER

First published in Great Britain in 1954 by Hodder & Stoughton

This paperback edition first published in 2014 by Mulholland Books
An imprint of Hodder & Stoughton
An Hachette UK company

1

Cover artwork by Andrew Howard
www.andrewhoward.co.uk

A CIP catalogue record for this title is available from the British Library

Paperback ISBN 978 1 444 76642 4
eBook ISBN 978 1 444 76643 1

To my Father with love

CONTENTS

CONTENTS

INTRODUCTION

Somehow I managed to miss the Saint during my formative reading years. As a schoolboy I was addicted to the thrillers of Hammond Innes, Alistair Maclean, Geoffrey Jenkins and Ian Fleming, and my fictional taste buds quickly matured (I like to think) when I discovered Raymond Chandler, Len Deighton and John le Carré.

It wasn't that I considered Leslie Charteris' Saint stories old-fashioned, or the product of a bygone 'Golden Age' – I did after all admire John Buchan and Nevil Shute – I just, due to a bizarre blind spot, didn't consider the Saint books at all.

My first experience of Simon Templar came in the persona of Roger Moore in the television series, probably the first series in 1962, which was compulsory viewing in my parents' house. I cannot claim that *The Saint* was required viewing because of my family's love of Leslie Charteris' books – I can never remember seeing one in the house – but rather because of my mother's love of Roger Moore, who had quite stolen her heart as a real (sort of) knight in shining armour in the television series *Ivanhoe*. As a consequence, the Saint appeared to me to be a modern day knight errant, the clunky armour and white horse being replaced with a white, and anything but clunky, Volvo sports car, which was of course far cooler.

And unlike Ivanhoe, who rarely seemed to stray beyond Sherwood Forest, the Saint got to visit a school atlas-worth of interesting and sophisticated locations – places which an unsophisticated Yorkshire schoolboy could only dream of. (It was only thirty years later as a cynical scriptwriter, I realised that the television Saint probably never got further than Elstree Studios in Hertfordshire.)

So for me, the Saint was a television, rather than a literary, hero and, I have to admit, one who quickly faced strong opposition in my youthful view, first from *The Avengers* (particularly the Emma Peel years), then *Danger Man, Man in a Suitcase* and even the deliciously camp *Man From U.N.C.L.E.* By the time the 1970s arrived, I had unconsciously wiped the Saint from my personal video tape of memories, if only to make room for newer stuff, and as a university student in those days, unlike these, that involved never admitting to watching television. And in any case, Roger Moore was now James Bond.

In the late 1980s, I became a crime writer with the legendary Collins Crime Club and the reviewer of crime fiction for the *Daily Telegraph*, yet in neither of these worlds did I encounter the Saint or his creator. However, being cowardly by nature (or realistic about my meagre talent), I had not 'given up the day job' which just happened to be working for The Brewers' Society, the trade association for the British brewing industry. It was through beer and pubs, not books that I was to finally appreciate Leslie Charteris and, in 1992, get to meet him.

It was in 1990, whilst researching the Brewers' Society's long-running corporate advertising campaigns, that I came across a file of advertising agency 'proofs' which had been earmarked for what we would call today 'recycling' but back then we just said 'the rubbish bin'. This particular file dealt with the 1960s, when the brewers had switched from claiming 'Beer Is Best' to a campaign which promoted the pub rather than the brew, under the strap-line 'Look In At the Local' and which used well-known personalities of the day, mostly footballers, it has to be said, but also, in one burst of press and television advertising, Leslie Charteris and his wife Audrey, extolling the virtues of the British pub (even though they only lived in the UK for half the year).

The file of agency proofs had been marked for disposal because (a) Brewers Society generic advertising had stopped in 1970 and (b) no one then employed at the Society knew who Leslie Charteris was! Except me; even though I had never read a Saint story. Here, whether I had read him or not, was a legend of crime writing, and so I refused to allow the file to be 'recycled.' (Today, I am proud to say, it survives in the archives of the library of the University of Warwick.)

When I learned that – thanks to the efforts of a true fan, Peter Lovesey – Leslie Charteris was to be awarded the Cartier Diamond Dagger for lifetime achievement in 1992, I had one of the press adverts from 1966 featuring Leslie and his wife reproduced as a photograph and presented it to him at the Diamond Dagger ceremony in the House of Lords. I think he was genuinely surprised and touched and also clever enough to realise that I was probably the one person in the Palace of Westminster that night who had never read one of his books!

And now, twenty years on, here I am writing this Introduction probably quite fraudulently and slightly shamefaced to be in the company of the genuine Saint fans doing the same thing in all the other volumes in this fabulous new edition.

The Saint In Europe collection of stories was first published in 1954. In terms of crime writing, that places it historically in the era of Ian Fleming's *Casino Royale*, Raymond Chandler's *The Long Goodbye* and Patricia Highsmith's brilliantly titled *The Talented Mr Ripley*. If nothing else, to survive in such distinguished company and still be in print almost sixty years later can be no accident.

As a complete 'Saint' virgin, the first thing which struck me about the seven stories in *The Saint In Europe* was how perfectly formed they were as detailed 'treatments' for episodes in – say – a long-running television series . . .

Imagine my surprise, then, when I discovered after a modicum of research on the jolly old interweb, that four of the stories were in fact the basis for episodes in that very first series of *The Saint* starring Roger Moore which hit our television screens in October 1962 (The Latin Touch, The Covetous Headsman, The Loaded Tourist and The Golden Journey) – coincidentally, my very first encounter with Mr Templar.

But this is supposed to be an Introduction to a book, not a review of a black-and-white television show, so do the stories deliver on the printed page? Certainly, they justify the title, for here is the Saint quite at home in Paris, Amsterdam, Juan-les-Pins, Lucerne and Rome, as well on the Rhine and in the Tyrolean Alps, all of which must have seemed extremely exotic locations to a British reading public only just (1953) free of wartime rationing.

And when touring Europe, the Saint didn't exactly stint himself; partaking of elaborate dinners and the finest wines known to humanity at every opportunity. No wonder his lifestyle, like that of James Bond, was attractive to an audience starved of luxury, but where James Bond was (in theory) a Civil Servant with a salary and a boss, the Saint had even fewer restrictions placed upon him. He was a man of independent means with plenty of time on his hands, free to travel unencumbered by wife, family, a mortgage or taxes, and with a charm which drew attractive, available, women to him like butterflies to honeysuckle. There could have been few male readers who did not envy such a hero, especially as such a carefree existence came liberally spiced with action and adventure at every turn . . . and the Saint didn't even need Bond's Licence To Kill when it came to the really rough stuff.

Sometimes it got very rough indeed. In *The Saint in Europe* three of the stories have particularly brutal endings, raising a few concerns about the Saint's moral compass, but then, with fine irony, the Saint never actually professed to be a saint, always keeping one eye open to his own advantage. In one of the stories though, The Spanish Cow, he is perilously close to coming across as a rather cruel gigolo in order to relieve an innocent, but plump, socialite of her jewels. (Actually Charteris leaves us in no doubt that the widow Mrs Nussberg is not just built for comfort rather than for speed, but is fat – very fat – and on the beach at Juan-les-Pins could easily be mistaken for a stranded Orca. Indeed throughout this collection, there are sideways references to fat men, who invariably turn out to be villains.)

Rescuing damsels in distress is one thing, but the attitudes shown to women in The Spanish Cow and in The Golden Journey have not dated well and a modern reader may prefer the Saint to pick on someone his own size.

The writing too has dated, from Charteris' curious mixture of overblown English – 'a gargantuan repast devoured with respectable deliberation' and all car journeys 'made at suicidal velocity' – to his use of Americanised dialogue – 'what's boiling?' 'My hot shot's outside' and 'What shemozzle are you up to here?' Yet this is only strange and unusual to me, someone who was brought up on the Roger Moore television incarnation, where the Saint is quintessentially English. Leslie Charteris, after all, lived for large chunk of his life in the USA and was, from the start, writing for an Anglo-American audience.

And there are times when the Saint's own dialogue resembles that of Bertie Wooster – 'Don't let him put you off your feed' and 'I should get a ducat for speeding'; but that is positively Shakespearean compared to the awful, laugh-at-the-foreigner French accent of a particularly shady character who declares at one point: 'Ze police 'ave learn nozing new about ze tragedy of your brozzer. But do not fear. Zey are very pairseestant. Soon, I am sure, zey will 'ave ze clue.'

Again, one has to try and remember that the Saint has been around a long time and the early novels were actually written in the era of Bertie Wooster and Lord Peter Wimsey – and indeed Hercule Poirot if one is searching for strangled French accents.

To expect modern-day political correctness from a book written sixty years ago is mere carping. Do these stories deliver what they set out to deliver back in 1954 (and much earlier), which was basically exciting, escapist entertainment? Yes, of course they do. They are also important in the historic landscape of crime fiction because the character of Simon Templar forms the perfect literary bridge between John Buchan's Richard Hannay (and E.W. Hornung's gentleman thief Raffles) and Ian Fleming's James Bond.

The Saint's buccaneering, devil-may-care attitude to law and order, total freedom from life's boring responsibilities and his uncanny ability to find skulduggery in the most exotic location, is surely every schoolboy's day dream and the Saint stories deliver full value. The schoolboys may have grown up, but they still day dream.

Mike Ripley

Paris
The Covetous Headsman

I

'I hope, Monsieur Templar,' said Inspector Archimède Quercy, of the Paris *Police Judiciaire*, in passable English, 'that you will not think this meeting is unfriendly.'

'Nevertheless,' Simon replied, in perfect French, 'to be summoned here on my very first day in Paris seems at least an unusual distinction.'

'The Saint is an unusual personage,' said Inspector Quercy, reverting gratefully to his native tongue.

He was a long, thin man with a long, thin nose, and even with rather long, thin hair. He had a solemn, anxious face and wistful eyes like a questioning spaniel. Simon knew that that appearance was deceptive. It was the Saint's business, in the cause of outlawry, to know the reputations of many police officers in many places; and he knew that on the record Inspector Quercy's instincts, if the canine parallel must be continued, leaned more towards those of the bloodhound, the retriever, and the bulldog.

'If you come here as a simple tourist,' Quercy said, 'France welcomes you. We have, as you well know, a beautiful country, good food, good wine, and pretty girls. They are all at your disposal – for you, no doubt, have plenty of those good American dollars which France so badly needs. But as the Saint – that would be altogether different.'

'Monsieur the Inspector is, perhaps, anti-clerical?' Simon suggested gravely.

'I refer, Monsieur, to the *nom de guerre* under which you

are so widely known. I have not, it is true, been informed of any charges pending against you anywhere, nor have the police of any other country requested me to arrest you for extradition; but I have read about your exploits. Your motives are popularly believed to be idealistic, in a peculiar way. That is not for me to judge. I only tell you that we want none of them here.'

'What, no ideals – in the *Palais de Justice?*'

Quercy sighed.

He gazed across his littered desk into the dancing blue eyes under quizzically tilted brows, and for a moment the lugubriousness in his own gaze was very deep and real. The sight of the tall, broad-shouldered figure sprawled with such impudent grace in his shabby armchair made a mockery of the conventional stiffness of the room, just as the casual elegance of its clothing affronted the hard-worn dilapidation of the furniture; the warm bronze of the preposterously handsome face seemed to bring its own sun into the dingy room, whispering outlandish heresies of open skies and wide places where the wind blew; and because of this man the office seemed more cramped and drab and dustier than ever, and the gloom of it touched the soul of its proper occupant. It was a sensation that many other policemen had had when they came face to face with that last amazing heir to the mantle of Robin Hood, when they knew it was their turn to try to tame him and realized the immensity of the task . . .

'I mean,' said Inspector Quercy patiently, 'that there are servants of the Republic, of whom I am one, employed here to concern themselves with crime. If you, as an individual, acquire knowledge of any crime or criminals, we shall be glad to receive your information, but we do not allow private persons to take over the duties of the police. Still less do we permit anyone to administer his own interpretation of justice, as I hear you have sometimes claimed to do. Furthermore I must warn you that here, under the *Code Napoleon*, you would not have the same advantage that you have enjoyed in England and America. There, you are legally innocent until you are proved guilty: here, with sufficient grounds, you may be placed on trial and required to prove yourself innocent.'

The Saint smiled.

'I appreciate the warning,' he murmured. 'But the truth is, I did come here for the food, the wine, and the pretty girls. I hadn't thought of giving you any trouble.' The devil in him couldn't resist adding, '—so far.'

'Let it remain that way, Monsieur. A vacation does every-one good.'

Simon offered a cigarette, and struck a light for them both.

'Now that I know how you feel about me,' he remarked, 'I suppose I ought to thank you for not trying to pin that Rose-pierre murder on me. It must have taken great restraint not to grab such a ready-made scapegoat.'

He had been reading the story in a newspaper at breakfast. The body of a young man identified as Charles Rosepierre had been found murdered in the Bois de Boulogne, the spacious park adjacent to the most fashionable residential quarter of Paris. There appeared to be no clue to the murderer, or even to the motive, for he was a respectable clerk in a shipping office, vouched for by his employers as honest and hard-working and by his friends and associates as being sober and amiable and impossible to connect with any shady acquaintances. He carried very little money, but he had not been robbed. He had left the office at the usual time on the day he died, apparently with no apprehensions, and it was understood that he was going to have dinner and call later on the girl he was courting; but he had not been seen since until his body was found a few yards from one of the roads through the park. There was no hint of a jealous rival, nor did anything in his open commonplace life give any

grounds to believe in a crime of passion; yet a passion of
some weird kind must have been involved. For what lent the
crime the eerie touch of horror that justified the space allot-
ted to it in the Press was the fact that although he had died
almost instantly from a knife stab in the heart, his head had
been severed from his body *after he was dead*, and was found
where it had presumably rolled a few feet away.

'I might have thought of you,' Quercy said, without the
ghost of a smile, 'if Rosepierre's body had not been found
two hours before your plane landed at Orly. When he was
killed and his head was being cut off, there is no doubt that
you were half-way over the Atlantic.'

'It was clever of me to arrive with a cast-iron alibi. You
really have no ideas about how I could have faked it?'

'I am satisfied, Monsieur, that that would be beyond even
your powers.'

'One day I must figure out how it could be done,' said the
Saint; and in some incredible way he made it sound
possible.

The Inspector grunted.

'You have not, perhaps, any more constructive suggestions
about the mystery?'

'I read a detective story once with a decapitated body in it,
in which the head was actually taken from an entirely different body, the object being to confuse the police and no doubt
the readers too.'

'The medical examination, in this case, proves positively
that the head which was found did indeed belong to the
body.'

'A big part of your problem, then, seems to be to find an
answer to why anyone who had already killed someone, for
whatever reason, should afterwards take the trouble to cut off
his head. It was not done to prevent identification, because
the head was left there.'

'Exactly.'

Simon gazed at the ceiling.

'Perhaps,' he said slowly, 'the name of the victim is a clue. Is it possible that you have in Paris some demented aristocrat who is still nursing a grudge for the treatment given to his ancestors during the Revolution? He has made a vow to track down and take vengeance on the lineal descendants of the revolutionary leaders who gave his forebears the radical haircut. Mistaking the name of this unfortunate young man for Robespierre, and having no guillotine handy, he—'

There came, perhaps providentially, a knock on the door, and an *agent* entered.

'*Mademoiselle North est ici, Monsieur l' Inspecteur.*'

'Good. I will see her at once. It is the sister of the murdered man,' he explained to the Saint.

'Then why is her name North?'

'She was adopted as a child by an American family. It is quite a story,' Quercy stood up. 'But I must not detain you any longer.' He held out his hand. 'Amuse yourself well, Monsieur Templar, and remember what I have told you.'

'I will do my best,' said the Saint, and wondered even to himself just what he meant.

2

He took a long look at the girl who was entering as he went out. She was American, obviously, in every outward particular, stamped unmistakably with all the details of dress and grooming that label the American product to a sophisticated glance anywhere. And since a pretty face is a pretty face in any country within the same broad ethnic limits, there was nothing about her features to mark her as conspicuously French by birth. She had softly waved black hair and clear brown eyes and a wide mouth which in happier circumstances, the Saint's instinct told him, could be generous in many ways.

Simon carried the image of her vividly in his mind as he retraced his way through the musty labyrinth of the upper floors and down the ancient winding stairway to the street. He stood at the gates of the courtyard for a few moments, indulging himself in indecision, and knowing all the time that his decision was already made. There was a sidewalk café on the other side of the boulevard. He crossed it and sat down at a table from which he could watch the entrance of the building he had just left.

And so, he reflected cheerfully, it was going to happen to him again.

It was true, as he had told Quercy, that he hadn't come to Paris with any intention of getting into trouble. He seldom went anywhere with the intention of getting into trouble. But trouble had that disastrous propensity for getting into him. It was, of course, originally Quercy's fault for ordering him to report at the Préfecture. The summons had been most courteously phrased, but it had been an order, just the same. The Saint had an unpardonably rebellious attitude towards all orders, especially police orders. That had prepared the ground. And then the Inspector had rashly proceeded to plant a seed. It was not that Simon could legitimately resent his warning, which had been most discreetly and even benevolently phrased; but nevertheless it had the ingredients of a challenge. The Saint had never found it easy to leave a challenge alone. And, unfortunately, there was an intriguing murder mystery immediately to hand for fertilizer. Even so, he might have been able to resist; but then he had seen the girl. It was harder still for him to leave a pretty girl alone. And hadn't Quercy himself invited him to enjoy the pretty girls? And so upon fertilizer and seed and cultivated ground, to conclude the metaphor, had fallen the warm rain of her presence; and the result was inevitable, as it had always been . . .

The Saint ordered a Suze, paid for it at once so that he could leave at any moment, and waited.

An hour passed before she came out, and he got up and threaded his way nonchalantly through the traffic. She stood outside the Palais, looking hopefully up and down the street for a taxi, and Simon timed his crossing so that he arrived beside her as one came by, and their hands met on the door handle.

They looked at each other with surprise, confusion, and incipient hostility normal to any two people caught in such a deadlock, the Saint playing his part exactly as if the accident was none of his making; and then he smiled.

'A photo finish,' he said. 'Shall we flip for it, or are we lucky enough to be going the same way?'

She smiled back – he had counted on the sound of a familiar accent to earn that.

'I'm going to my hotel – the George Cinq.'

'Mine too,' said the Saint truthfully, although his answer would have been the same whatever she had said.

As the cab turned along the Quai des Grands Augustins he knew that she was looking at him more closely.

'Didn't I just see you in that detective's office?' she asked.

'I didn't think you noticed,' he said. 'But I saw you.'

'Are you a reporter?'

He considered the possibilities of the role for an instant.

'No.'

'Are you connected with the police?'

Intuition, which had been whispering to him, raised its voice to a sure command. At this moment, in this situation, with this girl, the truth would gain him more than any fiction.

'My name is Simon Templar.'

'The Saint.'

She was one of those people whom he met all too seldom, who could hear his name and recognize its connotation without gasping, swooning, or recoiling; and at first he was glad to see she received it even without fear. 'The Saint,' she said, looking at him with no more than ordinary curiosity; and then the fear barely began to stir in her eyes.

'No, darling,' he said quickly. 'I didn't kill your brother. Even Quercy will vouch for that. He knows I was in an aeroplane over the Atlantic at the time.'

'Do you suspect me?'

'Did you do it?'

'I was on the Atlantic, too. On a boat. I landed at Cherbourg this morning. A policeman was waiting for me at the George Cinq.'

'Don't let anyone tell you these cops aren't efficient. They sent for me almost as quickly.'

Simon lighted a cigarette and gave his hunch one last retrospective survey, for the duration of a long inhalation. His mind was made up.

He said: 'This is on the level. Quercy had me in his office, giving me a solemn warning to keep my nose clean while I'm here. So I just naturally have an unholy desire to make a monkey out of him. I like you. And your brother's case is the hottest thing on Quercy's blotter right now. If I could break it and hand him the pieces on a platter, it'd be a magnificent moment. And I'm sure you want the case solved, whoever does it. So will you let me help – if I can?'

Her straightforward dark eyes studied him for many seconds.

She said: 'Thank you. I like you, too. But what can you do?'

'I may think of something. First, I've got to know everything you can tell me. May I take you to lunch?'

'Yes. But I've got to stop at the hotel first. They didn't even give me time to see my room.'

3

In the lobby, while she was asking for her key, a man stepped up beside her at the desk, removed a rich black homburg with a slight flourish, and said: 'Pardon, Miss North.' He extended a card. Looking over her shoulder, Simon saw that it said 'M. Georges Olivant', with an address in St Cloud.

'I 'ave waited for you all zis morning,' Olivant said. 'I am an old friend of your fahzer. I would 'ave met you at ze boat, but I was unable to leave Paris because of business.'

He was a stout man with a face that was unfortunately reminiscent of a well-fed rat, although the only fur on it was a carefully trimmed black moustache, the rest of the skin having that glossy pink patina which can only be produced by the best barbers. From the points of his polished shoes, up through his studiously tailored blue suit and studiously manicured finger-nails, to the top of his pomaded head, he exuded an aroma of Cologne and solid prosperity. He spoke English in an aggressive way which somehow gave the impression that he was extremely proud of his accent, which was atrocious. And just as the Saint had liked Valerie North at first glance, from the first glance he disliked M. Olivant.

'This is quite a surprise,' the girl was saying politely. 'How did you know about me, and how did you find me so quickly?'

'I read about your trip in ze newspapers,' Olivant said. 'So of course I am waiting for you. Eet was not difficult. Zere are not so many 'otels in Paris where ze Americans descend.'

She seemed to take the reference to a newspaper story on

her trip so matter-of-factly that a tiny line creased between the Saint's brows. Her name had meant nothing to him, and he thought he was aware of most celebrities.

'Then you must have known my brother,' the girl said.

'Alas, no. I am in Belgium, on business, when I read ze newspaper. It is ze first I 'ear of you bose since ze war. I mean to look for 'im, of course. But as soon as I return, before I can look, I read in ze newspaper about 'im again, and 'e is dead.' Olivant allowed an expression of grief to dwell on his face for a measured period of time, and then bravely set it aside. ''Owever, I come to place myself at your service. For finding ze murderers, we can only 'ope ze police 'ave success. But anysing else I can do . . . You will, per'aps, 'ave lunch wiz me?'

The girl's eyes went to the Saint, and Simon made a faint negative movement with his head.

'I'm sorry,' she said, 'but I've already promised . . . May I introduce Mr—'

'Tombs,' said the Saint promptly, holding out his hand.

The same kind of impulse that had made him introduce himself with complete candour to Valerie North now made him duck behind the alias which often afforded him a morbid amusement; but this time his inward smile vanished abruptly as Olivant shook hands. From a man who looked like Olivant, he had expected a fleshy and probably moist and limp contact; but the palm that touched his own was hard and rough like a labourer's.

Deep in the Saint's brain a little premonitory pulse began to beat, like the signal of some psychic Geiger-counter; but his face was a mask of conventional amiability.

'Mr Tombs,' Olivant repeated, like a man who made a practice of memorizing names. 'Zen per'aps bose of you—'

'I don't want to be rude,' said the Saint firmly, 'but my job depends on this exclusive interview. You know how newspapers are.'

M. Olivant made a visible effort to look like a man who knew how newspapers are.

'I am desolate.' He turned back to the girl. 'For cocktails, zen, per'aps? I 'ave look forward so much to zis meeting—'

'Excuse me,' said the Saint.

He strolled across the lobby to the little news-stand and glanced quickly over its wares. A guide-book with a shiny stiff paper cover caught his eye, and he bought it, and wiped the cover briskly with his handkerchief while he waited for his change. He walked back, holding the book by one corner, to where M. Olivant was taking his talkative leave of Valerie North.

'I come 'ere, zen, at five o'clock. I 'ave so much to tell you about your poor fahzer and what 'e does for us in ze Resistance before ze Gestapo take 'im . . . To sink I 'ave not see you since you were such a leetle girl!'

'I'll look forward to it,' said the girl self-consciously, letting her hand be kissed, and looked at the Saint. 'May I run upstairs just for a minute and see my room before we go?'

'Sure.'

As she left, Simon showed M. Olivant his book, holding it in such a way that the other was practically forced to take it.

'M. Olivant, would you say this was any good?'

Olivant took the book and thumbed perfunctorily through a few pages.

'Eet is probably quite 'elpful, Mr Tombs. So you don't work 'ere all ze time?'

'No; this is a special assignment.'

'Ah. I 'ope you make a good story.'

'At least it's a chance to travel,' said the Saint conversationally. 'But I don't suppose that means much to you. From what you were saying, it sounds as if you spent most of your time doing it. What sort of business are you in?'

'I 'ave many affairs,' Olivant said impressively, and seemed to think that was an adequate answer.

He held out the book, and Simon took it back again by the corner.

'Maybe you'd let me talk to you later, Monsieur Olivant. You should have some interesting things to tell about Miss North's family.'

'Ah, yes, eet is a most interesting story.' Olivant seemed curiously uninterested. He extended his hand briskly. 'Now, I 'ave anozzer appointment. Eet 'as been a pleasure to meet you. *Au revoir*, Mr Tombs.'

The Saint watched him go, with the sensation of that inappropriately calloused hand lingering on his fingers; and then he turned to the concierge and asked for a large envelope, into which he slid his newly-acquired guide-book, being careful not to touch the book again except by the one corner he was holding it by.

4

'Tell me,' said the Saint, 'as the most ignorant reporter in this town, what put you in the news? I mean, even before anything happened to your brother.'

They sat in opposite armchairs across a table in the tiny downstairs room of the Restaurant Chataignier, sniffing the savoury bouquet of its incomparable *homard au beurre blanc* rising from the plates in front of them, while the chef and proprietor himself uncorked a bottle of cool *rosé*.

'It sounds silly,' said Valerie North, 'but I was on one of those radio quiz programmes. I happened to know the answer to who was the painter of the Mona Lisa, and the prize I won was a free trip to Europe. They asked me what I planned to do with it, and I said it'd give me a chance I'd always hoped for to get to know my brother.'

'It does sound a little unusual,' Simon admitted. 'Hadn't you ever met?'

'Not since we were kids. We were born and lived here, till 1940, when the Germans were advancing on Paris. I was too young to remember much about it, but everyone was very frightened, and my father said we must go away. He wouldn't go himself, but he sent us with the wife of a neighbour – my mother died when we were very young. Somewhere on the road we were strafed by a plane, and the woman was killed. Charles and I went on alone.'

'Was he older or younger than you?'

'Two years older. But we were both children. Somehow,

presently, we got separated. I just went on, helplessly, I guess, with the stream of refugees who were trudging away to the south-west. Somewhere, after that – it all seems so far away and confused – I was picked up by an American couple who'd also been caught in the blitz. They took me to Bordeaux, and then afterwards to America. They were sweet people – they still are – and they hadn't any children, and they treated me like their own. Later on, they were able to find out somehow that my father had died in a concentration camp. They adopted me legally, and I took their name.'

'So, for all practical purposes, you really are an American?'

'I went to school in Chicago – Mr North is an accountant there – and now I'm a secretary in a mail-order house. And the only French I know is from high school.'

'Who was your father?'

'All I know about him is his name, Eli Rosepierre. And he was some sort of working jeweller.'

The Saint paused with his wine-glass half-way to his lips.

'Was he Jewish?'

'I think so.'

'I told Quercy there might be something in the name,' he observed. 'Of course, the name Eli fixes it. Now I get the Rosepierre. A literal translation of Rosenstein. I wonder . . . He must have been very brave or very foolish to stay here with the Nazis coming.'

'Perhaps he was only too optimistic,' she said. 'You know, I'd never thought of that, about the name.'

'Was he rich?'

'I don't think so. He worked very hard. But he may have been thrifty. I don't really know. As far as I can remember we lived in an ordinary decent way, not poverty-stricken and not specially luxurious.'

'But it's at least a possibility.'

'What difference does it make? Whatever he had, the Nazis must have confiscated.'

'If they could find it.'

'I suppose,' she said, 'you're looking for a motive?'

'There must be one. And I've got to find it.'

She watched him sub-dividing the last succulent pieces of lobster with loving regret.

'When did you locate your brother again?' he asked.

'Only a few months ago. The Norths had tried from time to time, without any luck. Last winter I thought I'd try just once more on my own. I had an advertisement translated into French and sent it to all the Paris newspapers. Of course, for all I knew, he might have been anywhere else in France, if he was alive at all. But, just by a miracle, he saw it. We exchanged letters and snapshots. He'd thought I was probably dead, too. And then, when I won that prize on the radio, it seemed as if everything was set for a real Hollywood ending.'

'I can see why that story would get a play in the papers,' said the Saint thoughtfully. 'And the correspondents of the French news agencies would naturally pick it up and send it back here.'

'They did. Charles's last letter said he was quite embarrassed about the publicity he was getting.'

'So, after that, anyone with an interest in the Rosepierre family, whether they read the advertisements or not, would know a good deal about both of you.'

'I suppose so.'

Simon shamelessly used a piece of bread to mop up the last delectable traces of the ambrosial sauce.

'Are you reasonably sure that this Charles Rosepierre *was* your brother?'

Valerie stared at him.

'He must have been! . . . I mean, he seemed to remember

the same things that I did. And people here knew him by that name, didn't they? And there's quite a resemblance – look!'

She took out her wallet and extracted a photograph which she passed to him. It showed a dark, rather delicate-featured young man with an engaging smile. Simon dispassionately compared it, detail by detail, with the face of the girl opposite him.

'There's a great likeness,' he conceded finally. 'It's probably true. I was only groping in the dark.'

'Here's another thing.' She was fumbling in her purse again, and she came out with a small round piece of silver like a coin. 'My father gave it to me just before he sent us away. It's one of those things that stand out in this disjointed kind of childhood memory. He gave both Charles and me one. And Charles mentioned it in his first letter answering my advertisement. He said he still had his, and he wondered if I still had mine.'

'That's pretty convincing.'

Simon took the piece of silver and looked at it, and a slight frown of puzzlement began to wrinkle his forehead.

'But if he was Jewish,' he said, 'why a Saint Christopher medal?'

She shrugged.

'Maybe he'd been converted. Or maybe he hoped it would bluff the Gestapo if they caught us.'

'Or maybe,' said the Saint in a far-away voice, 'it was just the handiest thing he had in the shop.'

She gazed at him blankly, while he examined the medal more closely and turned it over half hoping to find some inscription on the back. But on the back was only a little quarter-inch, indented square, much like a hallmark, except that the indentation was filled only with what looked like a cuneiform pattern of microscopic scratches which conveyed nothing to the keenest naked eye, if they had any significance at all.

And yet, for the first time, the darkness in which he had been groping did not seem so dark. There were vital pieces missing in the jigsaw which he was trying to put together, but at last he was beginning to perceive the outlines into which they would have to fit.

He was very silent while they finished the meal and the wine so that by the time he called for the bill the girl was fidgeting with understandable impatience.

'May I keep this just for a few hours?' he said at last, and dropped the medallion into his pocket without waiting for her permission.

'Have you thought of anything?' she asked.

He stood up.

'A lot of things. I'm not tantalizing you just to be mysterious, but they'll take the rest of the afternoon to check on, and I don't want to raise any false excitement until I've got facts to go on.'

He walked with her to the Boulevard Raspail, the nearest thoroughfare where they would be likely to find taxis, and only his quiet air of being so absolutely certain of what he was doing somehow forced her to control her exasperation.

'I'm telling the driver to take you to the Place Vendôme,' he said as he opened the door of the first cab. 'You'll find dozens of fascinating shops in all directions from there, which will keep you amused until your feet hurt. At five o'clock, wherever you are, grab another taxi and tell him to take you to a restaurant called Carrère, in the Rue Pierre Charron. Will you repeat that?' She did so. 'I'll meet you there at the bar. Until then you must not on any account go back to the George Cinq.'

'But why not?'

'Because as long as you're just wandering around the town the killer isn't likely to bump into you. At the hotel he knows where to find you. And I like your head where it is. I don't want it cut off.'

Her eyes grew big and round.

'You don't think it could happen to me?'

'I'll answer that when I know why it happened to your brother. Meanwhile, don't take any chances.'

'But, remember, I promised to meet that Mr Olivant at five-thirty.'

'I want to be around when you do it. That's what I'm talking about.'

Her breath broke in a gasp of incredulity.

'You mean you suspect *him*?'

'Darling,' said the Saint, 'this isn't one of those story-book mysteries, with half a dozen convenient suspects. I've known ever since friend Olivant showed up that he had to be a good bet. The only problem still is to find the motive and prove it on him.'

He closed the door gently after her and turned towards the next cab.

5

In a narrow street near the Odéon he found, unchanged as if the German occupation had only ended yesterday, a little stationery and book-shop which in those days would have earned a spot promotion for any Gestapo officer who had uncovered its secrets. Simon Templar went in and stood browsing over the titles on the shelves, while the jangling of the vociferous little bell hung on the door he had opened died away into silence. He heard a shuffle of footsteps at the back of the shop, and a voice that he recognized said courteously:

'*Bon jour, m'sieu.*'

Without turning, the Saint said in French: 'Do you have, by chance, a copy of the poems of François Villon?'

There was an instant's pause, and the dry voice said mechanically: 'I regret, but today there is so little demand for those old books.'

'"But where are the snows of yesteryear?"' Simon quoted sorrowfully.

Suddenly his elbow was seized in a wiry grip, and he was spun around to face the proprietor's sparkling eyes.

'*Mon cher Saint!*'

'*Mon cher Antoine!*'

They fell into an embrace.

'It is so many years, my dear friend, since I have heard that password!'

'But you remembered.'

'Who of us will ever forget?'

They held each other off at arm's length, and the years fell away between them. And as Simon laughed in the face of Antoine Louvois it was heart-warming for him to remember that this frail-looking grey man had been the redoubtable Colonel Eglantine of the *maquis*, whose exploits had perforated the intestinal tracts of Himmler's minions with even more ulcers than bullets; and he thought again that only a French hero would have had the sense of humour to hide his identity behind the name of a delicate flower. Those days, when the Saint's commission from Washington had been as tenuously legal as anything in his career, seemed very far away now; but it was good to still have such a friend.

'What brings you back, *mon cher ami*?' Louvois asked. 'We shall have much to talk about.'

'Another time, Antoine. This afternoon I am in a hurry.'

'Is there anything I can do?'

'That is why I came.'

Louvois relaxed into instant attention. As if not a day had passed, with a sobering of expression too subtle to define, he was again the sharp-witted, cold-blooded, efficient duellist of the last war's most dangerous game.

'*Je suis toujours à ta disposition, mon vieux.*'

'Was there in the Resistance a man named Georges Olivant?'

'What is he like?'

Simon described him.

'There were so many,' Louvois said, 'and under so many names. I do not recall him myself. I can make inquiries.'

'On the other hand, he may just as well have been a traitor.'

'There were many of them also, and many of them also have thought it wise to change their names. But that might be a little easier to trace.'

Simon put down the envelope which he still carried, into which he had put the guide-book with the conveniently shiny cover which Olivant had handled.

'On the cover of this book,' he said, 'are the fingerprints of this man. But cut off the top left-hand corner, which has my own prints.'

'That will make it very easy if his prints are on record.'

'You still have friends at the Préfecture?'

'Naturally.'

'I do not want this to become known to Inspector Quercy, of the *Police Judiciaire*.'

'He is a good man.'

'There is a personal reason.'

'*Entendu*. He will know nothing about it.'

'It is urgent.'

'I will close the shop and take the book over at once myself. I will have a report for you within two hours.'

The Saint fingered the medallion in his pocket.

'There is one other thing I can do while you are gone,' he said. 'Do you have an accommodating friend who is a doctor, who would have a microscope that I can use for a few minutes?'

'I can find one. Let me telephone first.'

Louvois retired to the back of the shop and returned in a few minutes with a name and address written on a slip of paper.

'It is all arranged. He is expecting you.'

'Thank you, Antoine. I will come back and wait for you. *A tout à l'heure.*'

'*A tout à l'heure.*'

Simon walked to the address, which was only a few blocks away. The doctor, a taciturn man with an old-fashioned spade beard, showed him directly into a small laboratory and left him there, asking no questions except whether the Saint knew how to operate the microscope and whether he required anything else.

The Saint placed the Saint Christopher medal face down on the platform, centred the square indentation on the back under the objective, and aimed the light on it.

As he adjusted the focus the pattern of almost invisible scratches sprang to his eye as legibly as a page of print.

He read the words so painstakingly engraved there, and then he lighted a cigarette and sat back on the stool and knew the answers to many questions while pictures formed for him in the drifting smoke.

He saw old Eli Rosepierre in his workshop, knowing that the Germans were coming, and too proud or too disheartened to run away, it didn't matter what his reason was, but wanting to save his children. And knowing that it was hopeless to trust them with such jewels and gold as he could lay his hands on, even though they would be lost to him anyway, but wanting to give them something that the invaders could not touch, for the future. And knowing that the children were too young to be relied upon to understand or to remember anything he might tell them about the modest wealth that was still secure. And faced with the problem of giving them the key to it in a form which they might understand some day, but which would be least likely for a child to destroy.

Anything on paper, of course, was out of the question. It was too easy to mutilate or deface, or lose; or a finder could read and take advantage of it. A tattoo might have done, but Rosepierre was not a tattooer. He was a jeweller.

And he had found a jeweller's solution.

Simon saw the old man working through the night with aching eyes, carving the most important achievement of his engraver's art. The etching of the Lord's Prayer on the head of a pin was a mere abstract diversion by comparison. This was his testament. On a medallion, because it was most indestructible; of silver only, because it would be least likely to attract a thief; of St Christopher, because it might disarm racial persecutors, and because it might be treasured more carefully – as indeed it had been . . .

The Saint took out the slip of paper with the doctor's address and copied down the words from the medal on the other side.

Then, more for idle physical distraction than anything, he wrote underneath the English translation.

There was only one weakness in Eli Rosepierre's ingenious idea. Why would his children ever have been likely to discover the minute engravings on the backs of their good-luck medals?

And in the next flash, Simon knew the answer to that one, too. There must have been someone whom Eli Rosepierre trusted, to whom Rosepierre had given an inkling of his scheme, whom Rosepierre had charged to find the children again, if it were ever possible, and tell them what to look for.

Olivant.

Simon thanked the doctor, who still asked no questions, and went back to Louvois' little *papeterie*. He paced up and down the street and almost wore himself out before the old guerrilla fighter returned. But the springy gait of the retired *maquisard* gave him his answer even before Louvois spoke.

'We have success, *mon cher*!'

Louvois insisted on unlocking the door and entering the shop before he would say any more.

'The fingerprints are those of one Georges Orival, *mon cher Saint*. He was a collaborationist, and for that he was sentenced to fifteen years in prison.'

'He has escaped, or more probably been released,' said the Saint. 'And he is looking very prosperous, under the name of Georges Olivant.'

'No doubt the *sale type* had plenty of blood money hidden away before they caught him.'

'He is now preparing to collect a lot more.'

Louvois stroked his chin meditatively.

'Perhaps that can be prevented. There are still many of us who do not think that imprisonment was enough.'

'*Ne t'en fais pas,*' said the Saint. 'His goose is practically cooked already. I personally guarantee it. I must go now and take care of him, but as soon as this is finished we must have our reunion.'

6

To his relief, although he had consciously tried to reassure himself that he had nothing to worry about, Valerie North was waiting at the bar of the *Carrère*, as he had instructed her. He ordered a Martini to keep her company while she finished hers, and paid the cab, but he would not talk even though the bar was deserted at that hour.

'All bartenders in this area speak English,' he said, 'and I don't want to risk even a chance of future complications. Our caravanserai is just around the corner, but I didn't want you to go there alone.'

As soon as they had finished, he steered her down the street to the Avenue George V, and turned her quickly into the George V Apartments, just before the hotel entrance. They rode up to her floor in the elevator of the apartment wing, and he piloted her expertly through the connecting passage to the hotel section.

'Don't ask me how I know these back ways,' he said. 'I couldn't tell you without incriminating myself. As far as you're concerned, it's good enough to fool anyone who's naturally expecting you to use the hotel lobby.'

He found a chambermaid to open the door for them with a pass key. Inside, she fetched up short with an exclamation, so abruptly that he trod on her heels.

The room was a shambles. Her two suit-cases were open, the contents strewn all over the bed, the other furniture, and the floor. But he was not seriously surprised.

'Did you try to unpack in a hurry when you ran up before lunch?' he inquired calmly.

'Of course not! Who would unpack like this? There's been a burglar here!'

She ran aimlessly about, rummaging among her disordered effects.

'Don't get excited,' he murmured. 'I don't think there's any harm done that a little ironing won't fix. If you'd been here yourself, it might have been very different.'

'I haven't got much jewellery,' she protested, 'but—'

'I expect it's all there,' he said. 'The one valuable piece was safe all the time.'

He held out the St Christopher medal.

She took it, and stared at him.

'You've got to talk now,' she said. 'If you don't, I'll go crazy – or do something I may be sorry for.'

'I'm ready now,' he said. 'Turn that medal over.'

'Yes.'

'You see that little square impression in the back?'

'Yes.'

'I put it under a microscope this afternoon. There's fine engraving in it. Here's a copy that you can read.'

He gave her the scrap of paper on which he had written down the inscription and its translation. While she looked at it, he cleared a space on the bed, and sat down and lighted a cigarette. He felt very placid now.

She read:

I, Eli Rosepierre, bequeath to the bearer, of whom this shall be sufficient identification, one half of the $50,000 which I have on deposit at the Chase National Bank, New York.

Eli Rosepierre.

'You see,' he said, 'you're moderately rich. Your father was lucky enough to have some assets that the krauts couldn't reach.'

Her face was a study.

'Then Charles's medal—'

'Must have been a duplicate of that one, leaving him the other half.'

She sank unsteadily into the nearest chair, ignoring the clothes which she crushed underneath her.

Simon laughed, and got up again to give her a cigarette.

After a full minute, she said: 'Where is the other medal now?'

'I expect your brother's murderer has it. But he hasn't had time to do anything with it. Besides, he won't be satisfied until he has both of them.'

'Why hasn't he done anything until now?'

'Because he couldn't. Your father trusted at least part of his secret to a friend whom he trusted, named Georges Orival. But Orival turned collaborationist, and after the war he was tried and imprisoned. He only recently got out, and he hasn't wasted much time. He introduced himself to you as Georges Olivant.'

'Olivant!'

'Apart from his obvious phoniness,' said the Saint, 'I knew I had something when I shook hands with him. He looks like one of the idle rich, but he has corns on his hands like a labourer. He didn't get them from pottering about in his garden. He's been doing several years at hard labour.'

The girl's hand shook a little as she drew at the cigarette.

'And he's waiting for me downstairs!'

'I'm sure it would take a lot to keep him away.'

'We must tell the police!'

'Not yet. We still haven't got enough evidence for a murder charge against him. And we still want that other medal. So we're going to meet him just as if you didn't expect a thing.'

'I couldn't!

Simon Templar gazed down at her with level blue eyes in which the steel was barely discernible.

'You must, Valerie, And you must go along with anything I say, no matter how absurd it sounds. You said you'd let me help you. I haven't done so badly so far, have I? You've got to let me finish the job.'

7

M. Georges Olivant folded the evening paper he had been reading and tucked it into his pocket.

''Eet say 'ere,' he said, 'ze police 'ave learn nozzing new about ze tragedy of your brozzer. But do not fear. Zey are very pairseestant. Soon, I am sure, zey will 'ave ze clue.'

'They know more than they're saying for publication,' Simon remarked. 'They told me so.'

He wanted to draw Olivant's attention to himself, not only to turn it away from Valerie North's pale stillness.

'So, you 'ave talk wiz zem?'

'And I've got a few leads of my own.'

'I 'ave read American stories,' Olivant said, 'where ze reporter is always a better detective zan ze police. You are per'aps one of zose?'

'Sometimes I try to be. Anyway, at least the motive for the murder is known.'

'Eet is?'

Simon took a leisured taste of his cocktail.

'Miss North's father – and the father of Charles Rosepierre – had a nice piece of change stashed away in a New York bank. He made a will leaving it equally between them. A rather unique kind of will. It was engraved in microscopic letters on the backs of two St Christopher medals, one of which he gave to each of the children. Miss North's medal has already been deciphered. Here's a copy of the inscription.'

He gave Olivant the scrap of paper, and tasted his drink again while the man read it.

The girl's knee touched his, inadvertently, under the crowded table, and he felt it tremble. He tried to quiet her with a comforting pressure of his own.

He had to admit that Olivant was good. The man's face did not change colour, and the dilation of his eyes could be explained on perfectly legitimate grounds.

'Eet is amazing!' Olivant ejaculated. 'Eet must be, as you say unique . . . Of, of course, poor Charles was killed to steal 'is copy!'

'You'd make a good detective yourself.'

'But eet still does not say, by '*oo*!'

'I've got ideas of my own on that score.'

Olivant's eyebrows rose in arches towards his well-oiled hair. 'What ees zat?'

'I've been talking to a fellow I met who used to be a big shot in the underground. We've got a hunch that there's some connexion with somebody that Rosepierre trusted, who went wrong and went the Nazi way – who may even have betrayed Rosepierre to the Gestapo. But if they tortured him, he must have died before he'd write them a cheque on that New York bank!'

For the first time Simon saw the crawl of fear beneath Olivant's sleek surface. It was no more than an infinitesimal twitch, instantly smothered; but it was all that he needed.

'Eet is too 'orrible to sink about,' Olivant said. He turned to the girl. 'Your fahzer was such a wonderful man. Everyone love 'im.'

'You can't think of anyone who might have turned on him?' she managed to ask.

'I could not think of anyone 'oo would be so bad!'

'My Resistance friend thinks he can,' said the Saint. 'Anyway, he's making inquiries.'

Olivant picked up his glass and drained it, and wiped his mouth.

'I 'ope wiz all my 'eart zat 'e succeed,' he said. 'But we make Miss North upset again wiz zis talk. I see it. Instead to remind 'er of 'er poor fahzer and 'er poor brozzer, we should try to make 'er forget a leetle . . . Now, I 'ave ze idea. I 'ave my car. Tonight it would be nice to drive out to St Cloud, to my 'ouse, where we 'ave a nice dinner, and per'aps 'elp ourselves to feel better.'

Valerie looked at the Saint desperately, but Olivant might have been anticipating the glance.

'Of course,' he said, 'if Mr Tombs is not engage, I am most 'appy if 'e come also.'

It was precisely what the Saint would have predicted, and the sheer cosmic inevitability of it gave him the same feeling of olympian omnipotence that a master dramatist must experience as he sees the last loose ends of his play falling into place with flawless accuracy in the third act.

'I think that's a swell idea,' he said.

He was afraid even then that Valerie would rebel, but terror seemed to have built up in her until she was gripped in a kind of trance that left her without volition.

They drove with Olivant at the wheel of a glistening new car, all three pressed together in the front seat, so that Simon could feel the rigidity of her body against him shaken by an occasional shiver, and knew that Olivant must have felt it, too, though the man chattered incessantly about nothing and Simon did his best to help keep the empty conversational ball rolling.

Once, while they were still passing through the Bois de Boulogne, Olivant broke off in the middle of a sentence and said: 'Are you nervous, Miss North? Believe me, I drive most careful.'

'I guess I'm just over-tired,' she said. 'Or else I'm catching a chill.'

'I know, you 'ave 'ad a shocking day.'

She turned to the Saint, leaning closer to him.

'Where are we?'

He hadn't wanted to refer to it, but he had to.

'The Bois de Boulogne,' she repeated after him. 'Where Charles was——'

'Please,' Olivant said quickly. 'For a leetle while, try not to sink of un'appy sings.'

'Now that it's come up,' said the Saint, in a very even tone that tried unobtrusively to transmit some of his strength to her, 'I must ask you one more question. About those medals, Valerie, that your father gave you and your brother. He didn't just give them to you to put in your pockets, did he? How were you supposed to wear them?'

'They were on silver chains,' she said expressionlessly. 'He must have riveted them, or welded them, or something. At least, I know that mine had no catch that you could undo, and it was too small to come off over my head. I wore it day and night for years. Finally when I got older I had to have the chain cut, because I had other necklaces I wanted to wear, and I couldn't wear that one all the time.'

Simon drew a deep breath.

'That's the last answer,' he said softly. 'That explains everything. Of course, he had to take the least possible risk of your losing them. And because your brother didn't have to be bothered about other necklaces, he never had his chain cut. He was still wearing it when he was killed. And all the murderer had was a knife. People don't normally carry wire-cutters, or a hacksaw, or a file, when they set out to commit a straightforward murder. It hadn't occurred to him that the chain wouldn't unfasten. And it was too strong for him to break with his hands, and too small to take off over the head. So the only way he could take it, on the spot, was to——'

'*No!*' the girl cried out shudderingly, and buried her face in her hands.

The car seemed to swerve a trifle.

'I am ashame for you,' Olivant said harshly. ''Ow you can 'urt Miss North like zis?'

'I'm sorry,' said the Saint.

But he wasn't, for the answer to that question, the mystery of why Charles Rosepierre's head had been hacked off after he was dead, had to be known. And he knew now, and there were no more questions. With certainty there came a lowering kind of peace.

Olivant's house was not large, but it stood well back in what appeared to be moderately spacious grounds, which looked overgrown and unkempt, about half-way up the hill from the river. The interior was sombre and smelled damp, as if it had lacked the warmth of human occupancy for a long time. Simon was sure that it had.

Olivant ushered them into the heavily furnished drawing-room and turned, rubbing his hands. He seemed to have recovered his overpowering confidence, and his smile was fat and expansive.

'Now,' he said, 'we are going to be 'appy. What will you 'ave? A cocktail? Sherry? I make you a drink, and zen I make dinner. I 'ave no servant tonight, but I am very good chef.'

'Living alone and liking it, eh?' said the Saint mildly.

'Yes. Tonight eet is just ourselves.'

Simon put out his cigarette. He could enjoy the full flavour of a situation as well as anyone, but he knew that there were occasions when to prolong the enjoyment for epicurean reasons alone could complicate it with unnecessary and unjustifiable risks.

He put a hand into his coat pocket as if reaching for another pack of cigarettes, but it came out with a stubby blue-black automatic.

'In that case, we won't put you to a lot of trouble, Monsieur Orival,' he said pleasantly. 'Besides which we prefer not to be drugged or poisoned, whichever you had in mind. All we want is Charles Rosepierre's medallion.'

'Are you crazy, Templar?'

The Saint smiled.

'I see you know my real name,' he murmured. 'I thought you would. You only had to ask a few questions at the hotel. It was a little harder for me to get yours, but your fingerprints on that guide-book were a big help.'

The man's face had turned red at first, but now the blood was draining out of it, leaving it grey.

'My name ees Olivant. Zis is an outrage!'

'It's going to be a worse one,' said the Saint cheerfully, 'if we don't get that medal. I'm sure it's either in your pocket or in this house somewhere. Now will you hand it over, or shall I shoot you in the stomach and look for it myself?'

Orival licked his lips.

'Eet is in my safe,' he said at last. 'Be'ind zat picture.'

'Go and get it.'

Orival dragged his steps to the painting and lifted it off the wall. Behind it was a small steel door. He manipulated the dial, and the door opened. He reached in.

He should not have been so conventional as to turn around with a gun in his hand. Simon was expecting it, and ducked. Orival's one shot went wild, but the Saint's did not.

Then the french windows burst open, and Inspector Quercy walked in.

8

'*Enfin*,' Quercy said stolidly, when the facts that he did not know had been told to him, 'Miss North has both the medals, and she should be able to claim the inheritance without too much difficulty. And we have this *canaille*, but not in the condition that the State would have preferred.' He prodded the body of Orival, alias Olivant, with his foot, and signed to the two uniformed men who had followed him in. 'Remove it.'

'The State ought to thank me,' said the Saint, 'for saving you the expense of a trial and execution.'

'It is lucky for you,' Quercy said, 'that I saw what happened and know that you fired in self-defence. We have, of course, been following Miss North all day, to see if the murderer might approach her. You see, we are not quite so stupid and useless as you would like to make us.'

Valerie North said: 'I hope you won't hold it against him. He's done so much for me. I'm afraid he'd never let me pay him, but at least I don't want him to get in trouble.'

'He has an irresistible advocate in you, *mademoiselle*,' Quercy said gallantly.

Simon glanced surreptitiously at the open safe, and then at the windows through which the two *agents* had just disappeared with their unlamented burden.

'By the way,' he said, 'just to complete the record, I think Orival still had the murder knife in his pocket.'

'Yes, we shall need that for the police museum.'

Quercy hurried out after his men. He was back in a few minutes, shaking his head.

'For once you were mistaken, *Monsieur le Saint*. It is not on him.'

Simon shrugged.

'Well, I guess he got rid of it.'

'It is not very important.'

Simon Templar agreed. What was important, to him, was that in those few minutes he had been able to transfer the negotiable contents of the late Georges Orival's safe to his own pockets. He caught the girl's eye, but she said nothing, and he knew that her sense of humour was coming back.

Amsterdam
The Angel's Eye

I

The Hollandia is one of the best hotels in Amsterdam. The best hotels everywhere exercise a proper discretion over the guests whom they admit to their distinguished accommodations. The clerk at the Hollandia read the name that Simon Templar had filled in on the form in front of him, and his brow wrinkled as he looked up.

'Mr Templar,' he said. 'Are you by any chance the Saint?'

Simon sighed imperceptibly. He knew that look. As a man who had rather a weakness for the best hotels, it was sometimes a little tiresome to him.

'You guessed it,' he said.

The clerk smiled with the utmost courtesy.

'I do not know if we have a room that would suit you.'

'I'm not too hard to please.'

'Excuse me,' said the clerk.

He retired to an inner office. In a few minutes he came back, accompanied by an older and more authoritative personage.

'Good afternoon, Mr Templar,' said the personage cordially. 'I am the manager. It is nice of you to come to us. But you do not have a reservation.'

'No,' said the Saint patiently. 'But I wasn't expecting any trouble. I'm still not expecting any. Not any at all. I'm on vacation.'

'Of course.'

'As a matter of fact, I only came this way to say hullo to

an old friend of mine, one of your eminent citizens. You probably know him – Pieter Liefman. He makes some of the best beer in these parts. But he's out of town, and won't be back till tomorrow or the next day. I just want to wait over and see him.'

'You are a friend of Mr Liefman?'

'We are what you might call brothers under the suds.'

The manager studied him frankly for a while, and found it hard to see anything that threatened the peace and good name of the hotel. The Saint wore his clothes with the careless ease of a man accustomed to the best of everything, and with the confidence of one who did not have to think twice about paying for it. And at that moment the keen corsair's face was in repose, and the imps of devilment stilled in the clear blue eyes – it was a trick of camouflage that sometimes served the Saint better than a disguise, and on those occasions almost made him seem to fit his incongruous nickname.

'I think we can find you a room,' said the manager.

So that minor problem was overcome, but not without starting a slight stir of curiosity that spread like an active virus through all levels of the human beings within the hotel, who were, after all, only human. Simon knew it when he came downstairs again after a shower and a change, by the studiously veiled interest of the staff, the elaborately impersonal glances and politely inaudible whisperings of the other guests in the lobby. The years had given him an extra-sensory perception of the subtle symptoms of recognition; but in the same time he had developed a protective tolerance for it. Let the speculations buzz: they could not embarrass him when he had nothing to hide.

For what he had told the manager was the simple truth. He had made the detour to Amsterdam in the course of an already aimless European vacation for no reason but the impulse to renew an old acquaintance and sample the products of the famous Liefman *brouwerei* at the source, and he had no thought of avenging any iniquities, robbing any robbers, or doing any of the other entertaining and lawless things which had made his name a nightmare to the police of four continents and given him the reputation which caused even tourists to stare furtively from behind their guide-books.

That this peaceful project was to be short-lived was not his fault – he himself would have added, with a perfectly straight face, 'as usual'.

He dined at the Lido, on a *rijstafel* of heroic conception – the taste for, and the art of preparing, a true Indonesian curry being one of the few legacies left to the Netherlands from their former East Indian empire – and it was not until his appetite was on the verge of admitting defeat that he had time to become aware that he was the object of more than ordinary attention from a table across the room.

There were two people at it, a middle-aged couple whose accents, as he had unconsciously overheard them speaking to the waiter, identified them as English, and whose clothes had a dull neatness that was worn like a proud *insigne* of respectability. The man had a square shape, with thinning hair, rimless spectacles, and a face moulded in the lines of stolid responsibility. The woman was plump and motherly, and looked as if she would be equally at home in a kitchen or a church bazaar. They looked most obviously like a senior employee of a prosperous business house, who had worked his way up from the bottom during a lifetime of loyal service, and his competent and comfortable wife. The only untypical thing about them was that instead of eating in the bored or companionable silence normally practised by such couples, they had been talking busily throughout the meal in low voices of which not a sound had reached the Saint's sensitive ears – except, as has been said, when they spoke to the waiter. Simon Templar, whose favourite study was the mechanism of his fellow creatures, had begun to theorize about what gave them so much material for conversation, as approaching satiety released his interest from food. It was not, he concluded, an affair of connubial recriminations, which might typically have disrupted a typical taciturnity; and yet the conversation did not seem to be made up of pleasant trivialities, for the man's air of permanent anxiety deepened as it went on, and once or twice he ran a hand over his sparse hair in a gesture almost of desperation.

It was about the same time that Simon realized, from the frequent glances in his direction, that he was somehow being made a major factor in the discussion.

He gazed out of the window at the twinkling lights reflected in the ornamental lakes of the Vondel Park and hoped that his impression was mistaken, or that they would soon find something else to argue about.

A voice at his elbow said: 'Excuse me, Mr Templar – you *are* the Saint, aren't you?'

He turned resignedly. It was the woman, of course.

'I suppose somebody told you at the Hollandia,' he said. 'But they should have told you not to worry. I've promised not to murder anyone or steal their jewels while I'm here.'

'My name's Upwater,' she said. 'And I did want to talk to you about jewels. But not about your stealing them. I've heard that you're really a good man, and you help people in trouble, and we're in terrible trouble. I told my husband it seemed like Providence your being here, just when this awful thing has happened. I said, "The Saint's the only person who might be able to help us," and he said, "Why should you bother?" and we had quite an argument, but I had to speak to you, anyway. At least you'll listen, won't you? May I call him over?'

She had already dumped herself in a vacant chair, and the Saint did not see any way short of outright churlishness to dislodge her. In the mellow aftermath of a good meal, such violent measures were unthinkable. And he had nothing else in particular to do. That was so often what got him into things . . .

He grinned philosophically and nodded.

'What's the matter with these jewels?' he inquired.

She turned and beckoned to her husband, who started to get up from the table, looking more worried than ever.

'As a matter of fact,' she said, 'it's only one jewel. A diamond.'

'Oh.'

'We've lost it. And it doesn't belong to us.'

'That could be embarrassing,' Simon admitted. 'But why should I know where to look for it?'

'It's been stolen.'

'Not by me.'

'This is a perfect blue stone,' said Mr Upwater, sitting down heavily, 'as big as the Hope diamond. It's worth half a million dollars in your money.'

2

'I work for a very exclusive firm of jewellers in Bond Street in London,' Mr Upwater explained in a ponderous and painstaking way. 'I've been with them myself for thirty years. The stone belongs to one of our clients. It is a magnificent gem, with a rather romantic name – the Angel's Eye. But being an old stone, it isn't too well cut. Our client decided to have it recut, which would improve its appearance and even enhance its value. As the oldest employee of the firm, it was entrusted to me to bring here, to one of the best cutters in Amsterdam, to have the work done.'

'And somebody swiped it from you on the way?' Simon hazarded.

'Oh, no. I delivered it to the cutter, Hendrik Jonkheer, yesterday. Today I went back to watch the start of the cutting. Mrs Upwater went with me. I'd brought her along for a little holiday. And – tell Mr Templar what happened, Mabel.'

'Mr Jonkheer looked Mr Upwater straight in the eye,' said Mrs Upwater, 'and told him he'd never seen him before and he certainly hadn't brought him any diamond.'

Something like a phantom feather trailed up the Saint's spine, riffling his skin with ghostly goose-pimples. And on the heels of that psychic chill came a warm, pervasive glow of utter beatitude that crowned his recent feast more perfectly than the coffee and Napoleon brandy, which he had not yet touched, would ever do. His interest was no longer polite or even perfunctory. It had the vast receptive serenity of a cathedral.

For just as a musician would be electrified by a cadence of divine harmonies, so could the Saint respond to the tones of new and fabulous adventure. And about this one, he knew, there could be nothing commonplace. Suddenly he was humbly grateful for his ambiguous reputation, for the little difficulty at the hotel, for the resultant gossip, for the extravagant bonus which it had brought him. Because in a few simple unmistakable words the prosaic Mr and Mrs Upwater had placed in his hands the string to a kite of such superlatively crooked design that its flight, wherever it led, could bring only joy to his perversely artistic soul – a swindle of such originality and impudence that he contemplated it with an emotion bordering upon awe.

'That,' said the Saint at length, with transcendent understatement after so long a pause, 'is a lulu.'

'I can't get used to it yet,' Mr Upwater said dazedly. 'He stood there, Mr Jonkheer did, looking straight at me just like I'm looking at you, only as if he thought I was a lunatic, and said he'd never set eyes on me before in his life. He almost had me believing I'd gone out of my mind. Only I knew I hadn't.'

'It's just like that story,' Mrs Upwater said. 'You must know the one. About the girl and her mother who go to a hotel in Paris, and the mother's sick, so the daughter goes out to get her some medicine, and when she gets back everybody in the hotel says they've never seen her before, or her mother, and when she goes to the room where she left her mother it's a different room, and there's nobody there.'

Simon nodded, almost in a trance himself.

'I know the story,' he said. 'It runs out that the mother had the plague, or something, doesn't it? And they got rid of her and tried to cover it up because they didn't want to scare away the tourists . . . But this is a new twist!'

'That it is,' said Mr Upwater gloomily. 'Only diamonds don't get any disease. But they're worth a lot of money.'

At last the Saint was able to control the palpitating gremlins inside him enough to reach for a cigarette.

'You're sure you went to the right place?' he asked.

'I couldn't go wrong. The name's on the door.'

'And you're sure it was Jonkheer you saw?'

'Of course I'm sure. It was the same man both times. The police knew him, too.'

'You've been to the police already?'

'Of course I have. First thing I did when I saw I wasn't getting anywhere with Jonkheer. They went with me to the shop. But it was his word against mine, and they preferred his. Said he was a well-known respectable citizen, but they didn't know the same about me. I almost got locked up myself. They as good as said I was either off my nut or trying to blackmail him.'

'Didn't anyone else see you give him the stone?'

'No. It was just him and me. I didn't take Mrs Upwater with me yesterday – she wanted to stay at the hotel and do our unpacking.'

'But if you say you gave it to him, Tom,' said Mrs Upwater loyally, 'I know you did.'

Simon picked up his balloon glass and rolled the golden liquid around in it.

'Didn't you get a receipt or anything?'

'Indeed I did. But this Dutchman swears it isn't even in his writing.'

'Could anyone else have disguised himself as Jonkheer?'

'If you saw him, Mr Templar, you'd know that couldn't be done, except in a story.'

'How about a black-sheep twin brother?'

'I thought of that, too,' Mr Upwater said dourly. 'I'm not a fool, and I've read books. He just doesn't have one. The police vouch for that.'

The Saint sipped his cognac reverently. Everything was getting better and better.

'And you would have vouched for Jonkheer.'

'I never met him before,' Mr Upwater said carefully, 'but I've known about him for years. Everyone knows him in the trade.'

'So you've no idea what would turn a man like that into a thief?'

Mr Upwater moved his hands hopelessly.

'Who knows what makes anyone go wrong? They say that every man has his price, so I suppose every man can be tempted. And that stone was big enough to tempt anyone.'

'Then,' said the Saint, 'the same could be said about you.'

'That's what he's afraid of,' Mrs Upwater said gently.

Simon sniffed his brandy again, watching the man.

'What does your firm think about it?'

'I haven't told them yet,' Upwater said dully. 'I haven't the courage. You see—'

'You see,' Mrs Upwater put in, and her voice began to break, 'they know Mr Jonkheer, too. They've done business with him for a long time. My husband's been with them for a long time, too, but he's only an employee. *Someone's* got to be guilty . . . They can't *prove* that Tom's lying, because he isn't; but that's not enough. If he can't prove absolutely that he's telling the truth—'

'There'd always be a doubt,' her husband finished for her. 'And with a firm like I work for, in that kind of business, that's the end. They'd let me out, and I'd never get another job. I might as well put my head in a gas-oven, or jump in one of these canals.'

He pulled off his spectacles abruptly and put a trembling hand over his eyes.

Mrs Upwater patted his shoulder as if he had been a little boy.

'There, there,' she said meaninglessly, and looked at the Saint with tears in her eyes. 'Mr Templar, you're the only man in the world who might be able to do something about a thing like this. You *must* help us!'

She really didn't have to plead. For Simon Templar to have walked away from a story like that would have been as improbable a phenomenon as a terrier ignoring the presence of a rat waltzing under his nose. There were people who thought that the Saint was a cold-blooded nemesis of crime; but altogether, aside from the irresistible abstract beauty of the situation that the Upwaters had set before him, he felt genuinely sorry for them.

His human sympathy, however, detracted nothing from the delight with which he viewed the immediate future. It was true that only a few hours ago he promised to be good; but there were limits. His evening, and in fact his whole visit to Amsterdam, was made.

He signalled to a waiter.

'I think we should all have a drink on this,' he said.

The half-conscious joy in Mrs Upwater's tear-dimmed eyes, to anyone else, would have been enough reward.

'You will help us?' she said breathlessly.

'There's nothing I can do tonight. So we might as well just celebrate. But tomorrow,' Simon promised, 'I will pay a call on your Mr Jonkheer.'

3

The name was on the door, as Mr Upwater had said, of a narrow-fronted three-storeyed brick building in a narrow street of similar buildings behind the Rijksmuseum: HENDRIK JONKHEER, and in smaller letters under it, *Diamantslijter*. From the weathered stone of the doorstep to the weathered tile of the peaked roof the house had a solid air of permanence and tradition. The only feature that distinguished it from its equally solid neighbours was the prison-like arrangement of iron bars over the two muslin-curtained ground-floor windows. Definitely it bore no stigma of a potentially flashy or fly-by-night operation.

Simon tugged at the old-fashioned bell-pull, and heard it clang somewhere in the depths of the building. Presently the door opened, no more than a foot, to the limit of a chain fastened inside, and a thin young man in a knee-length grey overall coat looked out.

'May I see Mr Jonkheer?' Simon asked.

'Your business, sir?'

'I'm a magazine writer, doing an article on the diamond business. I thought a man of Mr Jonkheer's standing could give me some valuable information.'

The young man unfastened the chain and let him in to a bare narrow hall. There were doors on one side and another at the back, and a flight of uncarpeted wooden stairs led upwards. On a hard chair beside the stairs, with a newspaper on his lap and one hand under the paper, sat a burly man with blond close-cropped hair who stared at the Saint woodenly.

'One moment, please,' said the young man.

He disappeared through the door at the end of the hall. The burly man continued to stare motionlessly at the Saint, as if he were stuffed. In a little while the young man came back.

'This way, please.'

The back room was a homely sort of office, the only possible sanctum of an individualistic old-world craftsman who needed no front for his skill. It contained an ancient roll-top desk with dusty papers overflowing from its pigeon-holes and littered over its surfaces, a battered swivel chair at the desk, and two over-stuffed armchairs whose leather upholstery was dark and shiny with age. There were china figures and family photographs in gilt frames on the marble mantelpiece over a black iron coal fireplace. The safe stood under another barred window; and, massive though it was, it would not have offered much more resistance than a matchbox to a modern cracksman.

Mr Jonkheer was a short bald man in his shirt-sleeves, with a wide paunch under a leather apron and a wide multiple-chinned face. It was obvious at a glance that no make-up virtuoso could have duplicated him. His pale blue eyes looked small and bright behind thick gold-rimmed glasses.

'You are a writer, eh?' he said, with a kind of gruff affability. 'Which magazine do you write for?'

'Any one that'll buy what I write.'

'So. And what can I tell you for your article?'

The Saint sat in one of the heavy armchairs and opened a pack of cigarettes.

'Well, anything interesting about your work,' he said.

'I cut jewels – principally diamonds.'

'I know. I'm told you're one of the best cutters in the business.'

'There are many good ones. I am good.'

'I suppose you've been doing it all your life?'

'Since I am an apprentice, at sixteen. I have been cutting stones, now, for forty years.'

'You must have cut some famous jewels in that time.'

A twin pair of vertical lines began to pucker between the cutter's bushy brows.

'Famous?'

'I mean, well-known jewels, that people would like to read about.'

'I have cut many good stones.'

This was manifestly going to make no revelationary progress. Simon said, as off-handedly as he could: 'You're too modest, Mr Jonkheer. For instance, how about the Angel's Eye?'

There was no audible sound effect like a sickening thud, but the response was much the same. In a silence that fairly hummed with hollowness, the diamond cutter's small bright eyes hardened and froze like drops of his own gems.

The Saint exhaled cigarette smoke and tried to appear as if he noticed nothing out of the ordinary. At last Jonkheer said: 'What about the Angel's Eye?'

'You know the stone I mean?'

'Of course. It is a famous diamond.'

'How are you going to re-cut it?'

'I am not re-cutting it.'

Jonkheer's tone was still gruff, but no longer affable. Simon looked puzzled.

'But you have it here.'

'I do not.'

'I was told—'

'You are mistaken.'

'I don't get it,' said the Saint, with an ingenuous frown. 'The fellow who referred me to you said positively that the Angel's Eye was brought to you for re-cutting only the other day. I don't mean to pry into your business, but—'

The other's steady stare was cold with suspicion.

'Who was this person?'

'It was somebody in the trade. I don't know that I ought to mention his name. But he was very definite.'

Jonkheer gazed at him for a longer time, with no increase in friendliness. Then he turned his head slightly and called: '*Zuilen, kom toch binnen!*'

The burly blond man who had been sitting out in the hall walked in instantly, and without any preliminary sound, so that Simon realized that the door of the little office had never been fully closed and the big man must have been standing directly outside it. He brought his newspaper with him, carrying it rather awkwardly, as if he had something underneath it. With his left hand, he took a small leather folder from his pocket and showed Simon the card in it. The card carried his photograph and an inscription which Simon did not have time to read, but he recognized the official-looking seal and the word *Politie*.

The big man, whose name was evidently Zuilen, was a very polite *politie*.

'May I see your credentials, please?'

'My passport is at the hotel,' said the Saint.

'Something, perhaps, from the magazine you write for?'

'I don't write for any particular magazine. I just peddle my stuff wherever I can.'

'You must have something on you, some evidence of identity,' said the blond man patiently. 'Please.'

He did not openly suggest that if none were produced the matter could be continued at headquarters. That would have been superfluous.

Simon produced his wallet, and watched interestedly while Zuilen glanced at the contents. The detective's eyes snapped from the first card that caught them to the Saint's face as if a switch had been flicked, but his manner remained painstakingly correct.

'Mr Templar,' he said, 'I did not hear that you were a writer.'

'It's a new racket,' said the Saint easily.

The blond man handed the wallet back.

'You would do well to search for your material somewhere else,' he said. 'There is nothing to interest you here.'

'Now wait a minute,' Simon argued. 'I'm not making any trouble. I was told on the best authority that Mr Jonkheer had received a diamond called the Angel's Eye to re-cut. I simply asked him about it. That isn't a crime.'

'I am glad there is no crime,' said the burly man stolidly. 'We do not like to have crime from foreigners, especially during the tourist season. Mr Jonkheer does not have any such diamond. Also he does not wish to be bothered. It is better that you do not make any trouble.' He held the door firmly open. 'Good day, Mr Templar.'

A few moments later, without a harsh word having been spoken or an overt threat having been uttered, the Saint found himself indisputably out on the pavement blinking at the noonday sunshine and listening to the rattle of chain and bolts being refastened on the inside of the old oak door.

'It was a lovely job,' Simon told the Upwaters. 'I never had a chance of getting to first base.'

They sat around a lunch-table in one of the crypt-like rooms of the Vijf Vliegen, that quaintly labyrinthine restaurant on the Spuistraat, where they had arranged to meet; although only the Saint seemed to have much appetite for the excellent *kalfoesters*, thin fillets of veal browned in butter and lemon juice, with stewed cucumbers and brown beans, which he had ordered for what he considered fairly earned nutriment.

'That policeman, too,' said Mrs Upwater indignantly. 'That Jonkheer really must have the wool pulled over their eyes.'

'Or else they're all in the swindle up to the neck with him,' Mr Upwater said bitterly.

'However it goes,' said the Saint, 'the place is pretty well guarded. And I haven't the faintest doubt that the Angel's Eye is there. They were so grimly determined to deny it. I could see it gave Jonkheer a good jolt when I asked about it. I bet they're still worrying about what my angle is, if that's any help to you.'

'It's there, all right,' Upwater said gloomily. 'Did you see his safe?'

'Oh, yes. In his office.'

'I didn't see it. I was taken right into his workshop the first time, and the second time I didn't get any farther than the hall. If I'd seen the safe, I might have been able to have the policeman make him open it.'

'His office is on the ground floor, at the back of the hall.'

'The diamond probably isn't there now, anyway,' said Mrs Upwater.

Simon took a deep pull at his beer.

'How big is this diamond?' he asked. 'You said it was as big as the Hope. How big is that?'

'About a hundred carats,' Upwater said. He put the tips of his thumb and forefinger together, forming a circle. 'About so big. It'd be easy to hide anywhere.'

Simon forked together the last remnants of food on his plate, and ate them with infinite enjoyment. Any lingering doubts that he might have had were gone. He knew that this was going to be an adventure to remember.

'I told you, I'm certain the Angel's Eye is at Jonkheer's,' he said. 'That's why the cop is staying on the premises. But I don't think it's hidden. I think they figure it's well enough guarded. And an old-fashioned conservative type like Jonkheer would have complete confidence in an old-fashioned safe like that, just because it weighs a few tons and he's had it ever since he went into business. He wouldn't believe that any up-to-date expert could go through it like a coffee-can.'

The man and woman gazed at him uncertainly.

'What good does that do us?' Mr Upwater asked at length. 'I'm no safe-cracker.'

'But I am,' said the Saint.

There was another long and pent-up silence.

'You'd *burgle* it?' Mrs Upwater said.

'I think you knew all along,' said the Saint gently, 'that I would.'

Mrs Upwater began to cry.

'You can't do that,' Mr Upwater protested. 'That's robbery!'

'To take back your own property?'

'But if you get caught—'

'If I only take the Angel's Eye, which Jonkheer isn't supposed to have anyway, how is he going to phrase his squawk?'

Mr Upwater clutched his wife's hand, staring at the Saint with a pathetic sort of devotion.

'I never thought I'd find myself siding with anyone about breaking the law,' he said. 'But you're right, Mr Templar – Jonkheer's got us by the short hairs, and the only way we can ever get even is to steal the diamond back, just about the same way that he got it. Only I could never 've thought of it myself, and it beats me why you'd take a chance like that to help a total stranger.'

Simon lighted a cigarette.

'Well,' he said, and his smile was happily mephistophelean, 'suppose I did just happen to take something else besides your diamond – by way of interest, you might say – would you feel it was your duty to tell the police about me?'

'*I* wouldn't,' said Mrs Upwater promptly, dabbing her eyes. 'A man like Jonkheer deserves to lose everything he's got.'

'Then that's settled,' said the Saint cheerfully. 'How about some dessert? Some *oliebollen*? Or the *flensjes* should be mildly sensational.'

Mr Upwater shook his head. He was still staring at the Saint much as a lost explorer in the Sahara would have stared at the approach of an ice wagon.

'I'm too nervous to eat,' he said. 'I'll be in a sweat until this is over. When will you do it?'

'On the stroke of midnight,' said the Saint. 'I'm superstitious about the witching hour – it's always been lucky for me. Besides, by that time our friend Jonkheer will be sound asleep, and even the police guard will be drowsy. I'm pretty sure Jonkheer lives over the shop and he's the type who would go to bed about ten.'

'Isn't there anything I can do, Mr Templar? I wouldn't be much of a hand at what you're planning, but—'

'Not a thing. Take Mrs Upwater sightseeing. Have dinner. Go to your room, break out some cards, and send for a bottle of schnapps. When the waiter brings it, make like I've gone to the bathroom. If anything goes wrong, you'll be my alibi – we were all playing cards. I'll see you soon after midnight, with your diamond.' Simon looked at his watch. 'Now, if you're through, I'll run along. I've got to shop for a few things I don't normally carry in my luggage.'

He spent an interesting afternoon in his own way, and got back to the Hollandia about six o'clock with no particular plans for the early part of the evening. But that state of tranquil vagueness lasted only until he turned away from the desk with his key. Then a hand smacked him violently between the shoulder-blades, and he turned again to meet the merry dark horn-spectacled eyes of a slight young man who looked more like a New Yorker than any New Yorker would have done.

'Simon, you old son-of-a-gun!' cried Pieter Liefman. 'What shemozzle are you up to here?'

The scion of Amsterdam's most traditionalistic brewery had spent some years in the United States, and prided himself on his complete assimilation of the culture of the New World

'Pete!' The Saint grinned. 'You couldn't have shown up at a better moment.'

'I've been out in the sticks,' Liefman said. 'I just got back in town and got your message, and I came right over to try and track you down. What's boiling?'

'Let's have a drink somewhere and I'll tell you.'

'My hot-shot's outside. We can drive out to Scherpenzeel, to the De Witte.'

'Good enough. The way you drive, you can get me back in plenty of time for what I want to do later.'

As Pieter Liefman needled his Jaguar through the sparse

evening traffic, with an ebullient disregard for all speed laws and principles of safety that would have had most passengers gripping the seat and muttering despondent prayers, Simon Templar leaned back with a cigarette and reflected gratefully on his good fortune. Pieter's timely arrival had made his project even neater than he had hoped.

'I guess you rate pretty high in this town, Pete,' he remarked.

'If you mean I should get a ducat for speeding, you don't know the quarter of it. They throw the books at me about once a week.'

'But in any serious case, I imagine you'd be as influential a witness as any guy could want.'

'Quit holding up on me,' Liefman implored. 'Is the Saint on the war-paint again?'

Simon began his tale at the beginning.

5

The return from Scherpenzeel, after a gargantuan repast devoured with respectful deliberation, was made at the same suicidal velocity, but so coolly timed that clocks were booming the hour that Simon had fixed in his mind as the Jaguar purred to a stop in the street where Hendrik Jonkheer plied his trade, but several doors away from the house itself. The short street was deserted except for one other car parked at the opposite end.

'I only hope you've figured this on the button,' Pieter Liefman said.

'I am the world's greatest practical psychologist,' said the Saint. 'Go ahead with your part of the act.'

He slipped out of the car and strolled unhurriedly down the street to Jonkheer's door. The building was dark and wrapped in silence. He turned the door handle experimentally. The door started to yawn at his touch, and no inside chain stopped it.

Simon stepped in, closing it swiftly and silently behind him. With a pencil flashlight smothered in his hand so that the bulb was almost covered by his fingers, he let a dim glow play momentarily over the inside of the frame. The chain was dangling, the hasp at one end still attached to it with fragments of freshly torn wood adhering to the screws, testifying to the inherent weakness of such devices which was no surprise to him.

He turned the same hardly more than phosphorescent

illumination around the hall, and at the foot of the stairs he saw the burly blond guard, Zuilen, lying on the floor, his wrists and ankles expertly bound and tied together and his mouth covered with adhesive tape. The big policeman seemed uninjured, except probably in his dignity, to judge by the lively glare of wrath that smouldered in his eyes.

Simon went past him without pausing for any social amenities, moving with the fluid soundlessness of a disembodied shadow.

The door of the back office was ajar, outlined with the faint luminosity of a well-shaded light within. Simon pushed it with his fingertips, and it swung wider without even an uncooperative creak.

Inside, he saw that the light came from a small professionally shrouded electric lantern on the floor beside the massive safe. The safe was open, and the means of its opening were evident in an assortment of shining tools spread on a velvet cloth in front of it.

Between Simon and the safe stood a man with a large handkerchief knotted loosely around his throat, obviously serving as an easily replaceable mask, who was in the act of stuffing a handful of small tissue-paper packages into his pocket.

'Good evening,' said the Saint, because it seemed as tactful a way of drawing attention to himself as he could think of.

He said it very quietly, too, in case his audience had a weak heart, but just the same the man spun around like a puppet jerked with a string.

The movement stopped there, because Simon was playing the beam of his flashlight pointedly on the gun in his right hand, to discourage any additional reaction. But there was enough general luminance, between that and the shielded lamp on the floor, for each of them to see the other's face.

Mr Upwater stared at him pallidly, and licked his lips.

'You weren't supposed to be here for an hour,' he said stupidly.

'That's what I told you,' said the Saint calmly, 'so that I'd know about what time you'd be here. Naturally you wanted to have comfortable time to do the job before I arrived, but you wouldn't want to be too long before, in case it was discovered too soon for me to walk in and take the rap. You did the ground-work very cleverly – getting me to come here this morning and case the joint for you, while at the same time establishing myself as a prime suspect. The only thing I was a little worried about was whether you meant to really let me do the job myself, and hijack the boodle afterwards. But I decided you wouldn't take that big a chance – you couldn't be sure that with so much loot in my pockets I mightn't yield to temptation and double-cross you. When you said yourself that every man has his price, you gave me a fix on your thinking.'

Mr Upwater's eyes were wild and haggard.

'You've got it all wrong,' he said feverishly. 'I was afraid you were just kidding me – that you wouldn't really do it at all – so I made up my mind to do it myself.'

'And not like any amateur, either,' said the Saint approvingly. 'Those tools of yours are first class. I suppose you wouldn't like to tell me how you got wind of the Angel's Eye being re-cut here? They were certainly doing their best to keep it quiet, to try and avoid having any trouble with people like us, as I could tell by the reception I got when I started to ask questions. It was nice work of yours to locate it; but you must have thought you were really in luck when you heard I was in town, all ready to be the fall guy.'

'So help me, Mr Templar, I told you the truth—'

'Oh, no, you didn't. Not from the word Go. I knew you were lying from the moment you said you delivered the Angel's Eye the day before yesterday and the cutting was supposed to start yesterday. Anyone who knows anything about diamonds knows that a cutter would study an important stone like that for weeks, maybe even months, before he made the first cut, because if he made any mistake about the grain he might break it into a lot of worthless fragments. And I was doubly sure that you didn't work for any big-time jewellers when you said that the Angel's Eye was as big as the Hope diamond and weighed about a hundred carats. For your information, the Hope diamond, good as it is, is only forty-four and a quarter. It's my business to know things like that, and it ought to be yours.'

Upwater swallowed.

'Can't we call it quits?' he said desperately. 'There's plenty for both of us.'

'Thank you,' said the Saint, 'but this time I'll be happy to collect the legitimate reward, with no headaches.'

'Nobody'll believe you,' Upwater said viciously. 'I'll say you were in it with me, right up to now.'

'I'm sorry,' said the Saint, 'but I've taken care to prove otherwise.'

There was a sudden rush of feet, and the lights went on. Two uniformed men stood in the doorway, with Pieter Liefman crowding in past them. Pieter put an arm round the Saint's shoulders and spoke rapidly to the policemen in Dutch, and Upwater wilted as he realized that the trap was closed.

Some time later, as they all went out into the street, with Upwater handcuffed between the two officers, Simon looked for the car that had been parked on the far corner. It was no longer there.

Pieter intercepted the glance.

'It took off when I came back with the flatfeet,' he said.

Simon read the mute entreaty in Upwater's white face, and shrugged.

'Okay,' he said. 'We won't say anything about Mabel. After all, she was the one who really brought me into this.'

On second thoughts, after he saw Mr Upwater's next expression, he wondered if that was quite the right thing to mention.

The Rhine
The Rhine Maiden

I

Simon Templar always thought of her as the Rhine Maiden for the simple reason that he met her on his way down the Rhine. He had never found the time or the inclination to sit through Wagner's epic on the subject, but he surmised that the Rhine Maidens of the operas would probably have been in keeping with the usual run of half-pint Siegfrieds and 200-pound Brunnhildes. The girl on the train was what Simon, in a mood of poetic fancy, would have liked a Rhine Maiden to be; and he didn't care whether she could sing top F or not.

Simon took the train because he had made the trip from Cologne to Mainz by boat before, and had announced himself a Philistine unimpressed. Reluctantly, he had summarized that much advertised river as an enormous quantity of muddy water flowing northwards at tremendous speed under a litter of black barges and tugboats and pleasure steamers, with a few crumbling ruins on its banks shouldering awkwardly between clumps of factory chimneys. Scenically, it had been scanned and found wanting by the keen and gay blue eyes that had reflected every great river in the world from the Nile to the Amazon, even though he found the ruins a little pitiful, as if they had only asked to be left in the peace of years and had been refused. Also Simon took the train because it was quicker, and he had unlawful business to conclude in Stuttgart; which was perhaps the best reason of all.

For the saga of any adventurer take this: an idea, a scheme, action, danger, escape, and perhaps a surprise somewhere.

Repeat indefinitely, with irregular interludes of quiet. Flavour it with the eternal discontent of unattainable horizons, and the everlasting content of an eagle's freedom. That had been Simon Templar's life since the day when he was first nick-named the Saint; and it was his one prayer that he might be spared many years more in which to demonstrate the pecu-liar brand of saintliness which he had made his own. With valuable property burgled from an unsavoury ex-collabora-tionist's house near Paris in his valise, and his fare paid out of a wallet picked from the pocket of a waiter who had made the mistake of being rude to him, the Saint lighted a cigarette and leaned back in his corner to be innocently glad that the lottery of travel could still shuffle a girl like that into the compart-ment chosen by the voyaging buccaneer.

She was very young – about seventeen or eighteen, he guessed – and her eyes were the bright greenish-blue that the waters of the Rhine ought to have been. She had pulled off her hat when she sat down, so that the unstudied symmetry of her curving honey-blonde hair framed her face in a care-less aureole. She was beautiful. But there was something more to her than her mere unspoiled young beauty, some-thing strange and startling that he could not define. She was the fairy princess that no man ever meets except in his most youthful dreams, the Cinderella that every man looks for all his life and knows he will never find. She was the woman that each man marries, only to find that he saw nothing but the mirror of his own hopes. And even when he had said that, the Saint knew that he had touched only a crude outline – that there was still something more which he might never be able to say. But because there seemed to be nothing of immediate importance in the newspaper he had bought at the station, and because even a lawless adventurer may find his own pleasure in the enjoyment of simple loveliness, Simon Templar leaned back with the smoke drifting past his eyes and wove romantic fantasies about the Rhine Maiden and the old man who was with her.

'This is der most vonderful river of der whole vorld, Greta,' said the old man, gazing out of the window. 'For der Danube der is a valtz; but this id der only river in der world dot has four operas written about it. Some day you shall see it all properly, Gretchen – die Lorelei, und Ehrenbreitstein, und all kinds of vonderful places—'

An adventurer lives on impulse, riding the crest of life only because he takes the wave in the split second where others hesitate. The Saint said, quietly and naturally, with a slight movement of his hand: 'I think there's some better stuff over that way. Over around the Eifel.'

The other two both looked at him; and the happy eyes of the solid old man lighted up.

'Ach, so you know your Chermany!'

Simon wondered what they would have said if he had explained that the police of two nations had once hunted him up from Innsbruck through Munich to Treuchtlingen and beyond, on a certain adventure that was one of his blithest memories; but he only smiled.

'I've been here before.'

'I know dot country, too,' said the old man eagerly, with his soft German-American accent faltering a little in his throat. 'When I vos a boy we used to try and catch fish in der river at Gemund; and vonce I got lost by myself in her voods going over to Heimbach. Now I hear der is a great *Thalsperre*, a big dam dot makes all der valley into a great lake. So maybe der is some more fish there now.'

It was as if he had suddenly met an old friend; the sluice-gates of memory were opened at a touch, and the old man let them flow, stumbling through his words with the same naïve happiness as he must have stumbled through the woods and streams he spoke of as a boy. There were many places that the Saint also knew; and a nod of recognition here and there was almost as much encouragement as the old man needed. His whole life story, commonplace as it was, came pattering out with a childish zest that was almost frightening in its godlike simplicity. Simon listened, and was queerly moved.

'. . . Und so I vork and vork, und I safe money and look after my little Greta, und she looks after me, und we are very happy. Und then at last I can retire mit a little money, not much, but plenty for us; und Greta is grown up.'

The eyes of the old man shone with a serenity that was blinding, the eyes of a man who had never known the doubts and the fretfulness of his age, whose humble faith had passed utterly and incredibly unscathed through the squalid brawl of civilization perhaps because he had never been aware of it.

'So now we come back to der Faderland to see my brother dot is a policeman in Mainz. Und Greta is going to see der vorld, und buy herself pretty clothes, und do all kinds of vonderful things. Isn't dot all we could vant, Gretchen?'

Simon glanced at the girl again. He knew that she had been studying his face ever since he had first spoken, but his clear gaze turned on her with its hint of the knowledge veiled down almost to invisibility. Even so, it took her by surprise.

'Why – yes,' she stammered; and then in an instant her confusion was gone. She slipped her hand under the old man's arm and rested her cheek on his shoulder. 'But I suppose it's all very ordinary to you.'

The Saint shook his head.

'No,' he said gently. 'I've known what it is to feel just like that.'

And in that moment, in one of those throat-catching flashes of vision where a man looks back and sees for the first time what he has left behind, Simon Templar knew how far he and the rest of the world had travelled when such a contented and unassuming honesty could have such a strange pathos.

'I know,' said the Saint. 'That's when the earth's at your feet, and you look at it out of an enchanted castle. How does the line go? – "*Magic casements opening on the foam of perilous seas in faery lands forlorn . . .*"'

'There's music in that,' she said softly.

But he wondered how much she understood. One never knows how magical the casements were until after the magic has been lost.

She had her composure back – even Rhine Maidens must have been born with that defensive armour of the eternal woman. She returned his gaze calmly enough, liking the reckless cut of his lean face and the quick smile that could be cynical and sad and mocking at the same time. There was a boyishness there that spoke to her own youth; but with it there were the deep-etched lines of many dangerous years which she was too young to read.

'I expect you know lots of marvellous places,' she said.

The Saint smiled.

'Wherever you went now would be marvellous. It's only tired and disillusioned people who have to look for sensations.'

'I'm spoiled,' she said. 'Ever since we left home I've been living in a dream. First there was New York, and then the boat, and then Paris, and Cologne – and we've scarcely started yet. I haven't done anything to deserve it. Daddy did it all by himself.'

The old man shook his head.

'No, Gretchen, I didn't do it all by myself. There was dot great man who helped me. You know?' He looked at the Saint. 'Und he is on this train himself!'

'Who's that?' asked the Saint cheerfully.

'Mr Voyson. Mr Bruce Voyson. He has der big factory where I vork. When I safe a little money I put it in his company because they pay so big dividends, und so there is always much more money; und I invest dot also, and so it all helps us. All my money I have in his company.'

Simon hardly moved.

'Sometimes I see him in der factory, und he has alvays something to say to me,' said the old man almost reverently. 'Now today I see him on der platform at Cologne. You remember, Greta? I think he is very tired with all the vork he does to look after the factory, because he is vearing dark glasses und he is very stooped like he never was before und his hair is gone quite white. But I recognize him because I have seen him so often, und besides he has a scar on his hand dot I remember so vell and I see it when he takes off his glove. So I go up und speak to him und thank him, and at first he does not recognize me. Of course he has so many employees in der big factory, how can he remember every one of them all der time? But I tell him, "You are Mr Voyson und I vork in your factory fifteen years und I invest all my money in your company, und I vant to thank you that now I can retire and go home." So he shakes hands with me, und then he is so busy that he has to go away. But he is on der train, too.'

'You put all your money in Voyson's company?' repeated the Saint, with a sudden weariness.

The old man nodded.

'Dot is how I mean, I didn't do it all by myself. If I hadn't done that I should've had to vork some more years.'

Simon Templar's eyes fell to the newspaper on his knee. For it was on that day that the collapse of the Voyson Plastics Company was exposed by the sudden disappearance of the President, and ruined investors learned for the first time that the rock on which they had been lured to found their fortunes was nothing but a quicksand. Even the local sheet which the Saint had bought devoted an entire column to the first reve-lations of the crack-up.

Simon drew a slow breath as if he had received a physical

blow. There was nothing very novel about the story; there never will be anything very novel about these things, except for the scale of the disaster; and certainly there was nothing very novel about it in the Saint's experience. But his heart went oddly heavy. For a second he thought that he would rather anyone but himself should bring the tragedy – anyone who hadn't seen what he had seen, who hadn't been taken into the warmth and radiance of the enchanted castle that had been opened to him. But he knew that the old man would have to know, sooner or later. And the girl would have to know.

He held out the paper.

'Maybe you haven't read any news lately,' he said quietly, and turned away to the window because he preferred not to see.

The lottery of travel had done a good job. It reached out into the world and threw lives and stories together, shuffled them in a brief instant, and then left them altered for ever. An adventurer, a Rhine Maiden, an old man. Hope, romance, a crooked company promoter, a scrap of cheap newsprint, tragedy. Perhaps every route that carries human freight is the same, only one doesn't often see the working of it. Human beings conquering and falling and rising again, each in his own trivial little play, in the inscrutable loneliness which everything human makes for itself wherever crowds mingle and never know each other's names. Simon Templar had loved the lottery for its own sake, because it was a gamble where such infinitely exciting things could happen; but now he thought that it looked on its handiwork and sneered. He could have punched it on the nose.

After a long time the old man was speaking to him.

'It isn't true. It couldn't be true. Der great big company like dot couldn't break down!'

Simon looked into the dazed honest eyes.

'I'm afraid it must be true,' he said steadily.

'But I spoke to him only a little vhile ago. I thanked him. Und he shook hands with me.' The old man's voice was pleading tremulously for the light that wasn't there. 'No man could have acted a lie like dot . . . Vait! I go to him myself, and he'll tell me it isn't true.'

He stood up and dragged himself shakily to the door, holding the luggage rack to support himself.

Simon filled his lungs.

He fell back into the reality of it with a jolt like a plunge into cold water, which left him braced and tingling. Mentally, he shook himself like a dog. He realized that the fragment of drama which had been flung before him had temporarily obscured everything else; that because the tragedy had struck two people who had given him a glimpse of a rare loveliness that he had forgotten for many years, he had taken their catastrophe for his own. But they were only two of many thousands. One never feels the emotion of these things, except academically, until it touches the links of one's own existence. Life was life. It had happened before, and it would happen again. Of the many crooked financiers whom the Saint had known to their loss, there was scarcely one whose victims he had ever considered. But Bruce Voyson was actually on the train, and he must have been carrying some wealth with him, and the old man knew what he looked like.

The girl was rising to follow, but Simon put his hands on her shoulders and held her back.

'I'll look after him,' he said. 'Perhaps you'd better stay here.'

He swung himself through the door and went waiting down the corridor, long-limbed and alert. A man like Bruce Voyson would be fair game for any adventurer; and it was in things like that that the Saint was most at home. The fact that he could be steered straight to his target by a man who could really recognize the financier when he saw him, in spite of his disguise, was a miracle too good to miss. Action, swift and spontaneous and masterly, was more in the Saint's line than a contemplation of the brutal ironies of Fate; and the prospect of it took his mind resiliently away from gloom.

He followed the old man along the train at a leisured distance. At each pause where the old man stopped to peer into a compartment the Saint stopped also and lounged against the side, patient as a stalking tiger. Some time later he pushed into another carriage and found himself in the dining-car, for it was an early train with provision for the breakfasts of late-rising travellers. The old man was standing over a table half-way down; and one glance was enough to show that he had found his quarry.

Simon sank unnoticed into the adjoining booth. In a panel of mirror on the opposite side he could see the man who must have been Bruce Voyson – a thin dowdily dressed man with the almost white hair and tinted glasses which the old German had described. The glasses seemed to hide most of the sallow face, so that the line of the thin straight mouth was the only expressive feature to be seen.

The old German was speaking.

'Mr Voyson, I'm asking you a question und I vant an answer. Is it true dot your company is smashed?'

Voyson hesitated for a moment, as if he was not quite sure whether he had heard the question correctly. And then, as he seemed to make up his mind, his gloved fingers twisted together on the table in front of him.

'Absolute nonsense,' he said shortly. 'I don't know what you're talking about.'

The old man swallowed.

'Then vhy is it, Mr Voyson, dot der paper here says dot it is all smashed, und everyone vants to know where you are?'

'What paper is that?' demanded Voyson; but there was a harsh twitch in his voice.

The old man dropped it on the table.

'Dot's der paper. If you don't understand Cherman I translate it for you. It says: "Von of der biggest swindle in history was yesterday in Maxton, Ohio, exposed—"'

Voyson bit the corner of his mouth, then swung round.

'Well, what about it?'

'But, Mr Voyson, you cannot speak of it like dot. You

cannot realize vat it means. If it is true dot der money is all gone . . . You don't understand. All my life I vork and vork, und I safe money, und I put it all in your company. It cannot be true dot all my money is gone – dot all my life I have vork for nothing—'

'Suppose it is gone?' snapped Voyson. 'There are plenty of others in the same boat.' He sighed. 'It's all in the luck of the game.'

The old man swayed and steadied himself heavily.

'Luck?' he said hoarsely. 'You talk to me of luck? When I am ruined, und it says here dot it vas all a swindle – dot you are nodding but a criminal—'

Voyson's fist hit the table.

'Now you listen to me,' he rasped. 'We're not in America now – either of us. If you've got any complaints you can take me back to Ohio first and then go ahead and prove I swindled you. That'll be soon enough for you to start shooting off your mouth about criminals. Now, what d'you think you're going to do about it? Think it over. And get the hell out of here while you do your thinking, or I'll call the guard and have you thrown off the train!'

The Saint's muscles hardened, and relaxed slowly. His dark head settled back almost peacefully on the upholstery behind him; but the wraith of a smile on his lips had the grim glitter of polished steel. A steward hovered over him, and he ordered a sandwich which he did not want without turning his head.

Minutes later, or it might have been hours, he saw his travelling acquaintance going past him. The old man looked neither to right nor left. His faded eyes stared sightlessly ahead, glazed with a terrible stony emptiness. His big toil-worn hands, which could have picked Voyson up and broken him across one knee, hung listlessly at his sides. His feet slouched leadenly, as if they were moved by a conscious effort of will.

Simon sat on. After another few minutes Voyson paid his

bill and went past, walking jerkily. His coat was rucked up on one side, and Simon saw the tell-tale bulge on the right hip before it was straightened.

The Saint spread coins thoughtfully on the table to cover the price of his sandwich. His eyes ran over the selection of condiments which had come with it, and almost absentmindedly he dropped the pepper-pot into his pocket. Then he picked up the sandwich as he stood up, took a bite from it, and sauntered out with it in his hand.

At the entrance of the next coach something caught at the tail of his eye, and he stopped abruptly. The door at the side was open, and the bowed figure of the old German stood framed in the oblong, looking out. The broad, rounded shoulders had a deathly rigidity. While Simon looked, the gnarled hands tightened on the handrails by which the figure held itself upright, stretching the skin white over the knuckles; then they let go.

Simon covered the distance in two lightning strides and dragged him back. A train passing in the opposite direction blasted his ears with its sudden crashing clamour, and went clattering by in a gale of acrid wind. The old man fought him blindly, but Simon's lean strength pinned him against the bulk-head. The noise outside whisked by and vanished again as suddenly as it had come, giving place to the subdued rhythmic mutter of their own passage.

'Don't be a fool!' snapped the Saint metallically. 'What sort of help is that going to be to Greta?'

The old man's struggling arms went limp gradually. He gazed dumbly back, trying to understand. His throat moved twice, convulsively, before his voice came.

'Dot's right . . . dot's right . . . I must look after Greta. Und she is so young . . .'

Simon let him go, and he went weakly past, around the corner into the main corridor.

The Saint lighted a cigarette and inhaled deeply. It had been close enough . . . And once again he gave himself that mental shake, feathering himself down to that ice-cold clarity of purpose in which any adventurer's best work must be done. It was a tough break for the old Dutchman, but Simon couldn't keep his mind solely on that. He didn't want to. Such distractions as the rescuing of potential damn-fool suicides from sticky ends disturbed the even course of buccaneering. Voyson was on the train; and the ungodly prospered only that a modern pirate might loot them.

A little way farther down the carriage Simon found the financier sitting in a first-class compartment by himself. The Saint eased back the door and stepped through, sliding it shut behind him. He stood with his sandwich in one hand and his cigarette in the other, balancing himself lightly against the sway.

'A word with you,' he said.

3

Voyson looked up.

'Who are you?' he demanded irritably.

'*New York Herald Tribune*, European editor,' said the Saint coolly and mendaciously. 'I want an interview. Mind if I sit down?'

He took a seat next to the financier as if he had never considered the possibility of a refusal.

'Why do you think I should have anything to tell you?'

The Saint smiled.

'You're Bruce Voyson, aren't you?' He touched the man's head, then looked at his fingertips. 'Yes, I thought so. It's wonderful what a difference a little powder will make. And those dark glasses help a lot, too.' His fingers patted one of Voyson's hands. 'Besides, if there's going to be any argument, there ought to be a scar here which would settle it. Take that glove off and show me that you haven't got a scar, and I'll apologize and go home.'

'I've no statement to make,' said Voyson coldly, though the ragged edge of his nerves showed in the shift of his eyes and the flabby movement of his hands. 'When I have, you'll get it. Now, d'you mind getting out?'

'A bad line,' murmured the Saint reprovingly. 'Very bad. Always give the papers a break, and then they'll see you get a good seat when the fireworks go off.' He put his left arm round the financier's shoulders, and patted the man's chest in a brotherly manner with his right hand. 'Come along, now,

Mr Voyson – let's have the dope. What's the inside story about your company?'

Voyson shook him off savagely.

'I've got no statement to make, I tell you! The whole story's a rigmarole of lies. When I get back I'll sue every paper that's printed it – and that goes for yours, too! Now get out – d'you hear?'

'Spoken like a man,' drawled the Saint appreciatively. 'We ought to have had a newsreel here to record it. Now, about this trip of yours—'

'Where did you get that?' whispered Voyson.

His eyes were frozen on the booklet of coloured papers which the Saint was skimming through. Simon glanced up and back to them again.

'Out of your pocket,' he answered calmly. 'Just put me down as inquisitive.'

He turned the leaflets interestedly, examining them one by one until he came to the end. Then he replaced them in their neat folder, snapped the elastic, and stowed it away in his own pocket.

'Destination Batavia, I see,' he remarked genially. 'Well, I'm sure you'll be able to straighten everything out when you get back to Maxton. Putting duty before everything else and going home by the shortest route, too. Indonesia is on the direct line to Ohio from here – via Australia. Are you taking in Australia? You oughtn't to miss the wallabies ... You certainly are going to have a nice long voyage to recover from the strain of trying to save your shareholders' money. And, by the way, there are quite a lot of extradition difficulties from Indonesia to the United States when a guy is wanted for your particular kind of nastiness, aren't there?'

Voyson rubbed his chin with a shaking hand. His gaze was fixed on the Saint with the quivering intensity of a guinea-pig hypnotized by a snake.

'Picked my pocket, eh?' he got out harshly. 'I'll see your editor hears about that. I'll have you arrested!'

He reached for the communication cord. Simon tilted his head back and half-closed his eyes.

'What a story!' he breathed ecstatically. 'Of course it'll delay you a bit having to stay on in Germany to make the charge and see it all through. But if you think it's worth it, I do. It'd be front-page stuff!'

Voyson sank down again.

'Will you get out of my compartment?' he grated. 'I've stood as much from you as I intend to—'

'But you haven't stood as much from me as I've got waiting for you, brother,' said the Saint.

His eyes opened suddenly, very clear and blue and reckless, like sapphires with steel rapier-points behind them. He smiled.

'I'm here on business, Bruce,' he said in the same gentle voice with the tang of bared sword-blades behind its melting smoothness. 'I won't deceive you any longer – the *Herald Tribune* only knows me from the comic section. And I don't like you, brother. I never have cared much for your line of business, anyway, and the way you spoke to that poor old man in the dining-car annoyed me. Remember him? He was on the point of chucking himself off this train under another one just now when I happened along. Somehow, my pet, I don't think it would have distressed me nearly so much if you'd had the same idea.'

'Who are you?' asked Voyson huskily.

'I am the Saint – you may have heard of me. Just a twentieth-century privateer. In my small way I try to put right a few of the things that are wrong with this cock-eyed world, and clean up some of the excrescences I come across. You come into the category, comrade. You must be carrying quite a tidy bit of boodle along to comfort you in your exile, and I think I could spend it much more amusingly than you—'

Voyson's lips whitened. His hand slipped behind him, and Simon looked down at the barrel of an automatic levelled into the centre of his chest. Only the Saint's eyebrows moved.

'You've been getting notions from some of these gangster pictures,' he said. 'May I go on with my eating?'

He put the sandwich on his knee and lifted off the top slice of bread. Then he felt in his pocket for the pepperpot. The perforations in the top seemed inadequate, and he unscrewed the cap.

Voyson squinted at him.

'That makes it easier to deal with you,' he said; and then a cloud of pepper struck him squarely in the face.

It came with a crisp upward fling that drove the powder straight up his nostrils and up under the shield of his glasses into his eyes. He choked and gasped, and in the same instant his gun was struck aside and detached skilfully from his fingers.

Minutes of streaming agony passed before his tortured vision returned. While he wept with the stinging pain of it his pockets were rifled again, this time without any attempt at stealth. Once he tried to rise, and was pushed back like a child. He huddled away and waited impotently for the blindness to wear off.

When he looked up the Saint was still there, sitting on the seat opposite him with a handkerchief over his face and a litter of papers sorted out on his lap and overflowing on either side. The window had been lowered so that the draught could clear the air.

'You crook!' Voyson moaned.

'Well, well, well!' murmured the Saint amiably. 'So the little man's come to the surface again. Bad business, that hay fever of yours. Speaking as one crook to another, Bruce, you ought to give up gun-play until you're cured. Sneezing spoils the aim.'

He removed the handkerchief from his face, sniffed the air

cautiously and tucked the silk square back in his pocket. Then he began to gather up the papers he had been investigating.

'I can only find ninety thousand dollars in cash,' he said. 'That's not a lot of booty out of a five-million-dollar swindle. But I see there are notes of two-million-dollar transfers to the Asiatic Bank of Batavia; so maybe you didn't do so badly out of it. I wish we could touch some of that bank account, though.'

He enveloped the documents deliberately in the wallet from which he had taken them, and tossed it back. Voyson's bloodshot glare steadied itself.

'I'll see that you don't get away with this,' he snarled.

'Tell me how,' invited the Saint, but his smile was still a glitter of clean-cut marble.

'Wait till we get to Mainz. There are plenty of people on this train. What are you going to do – walk me out of the station under that gun in broad daylight? I'd like to see you do it. I'll call your bluff!'

'Still hankering for that publicity?'

'I've got to have those tickets,' said Voyson, with his chest labouring. 'And my money. I've got to get to Batavia. You won't stop me! I shan't have to stay behind to make any charges. Your having a gun will be enough – and my money and tickets on you. I know the numbers of all those bills, and the tickets are signed with my name. The police'll be glad to see you!' Voyson's hands were clenching and twitching spasmodically. 'I think I read about you being in trouble here some time ago, didn't I?'

Simon said nothing, and Voyson's voice picked up. It grew louder than it need have done, almost as if the financier was trying to bolster up his own confidence with the sound of it.

'The German police wanted you pretty badly then! You're the Saint, eh? It's a good thing you told me.'

'You make things very difficult, brother,' said the Saint.

His quietness was unruffled, almost reflective; yet to any man in his senses that very quietness should have flared with warnings. Voyson was beyond seeing them. He leaned forward with the red pin-points in his stare glittering.

'I want it to,' he raved. 'You've come to the wrong man with your nonsense. I'll give you thirty seconds to hand back my tickets—'

'One moment,' said the Saint.

His soft incisiveness floated like a white-hot filament across the other's babble of speech; and suddenly Voyson saw the coldness of his eyes and went silent.

'You're reminding me of things that I haven't remembered for a long time,' said the Saint soberly.

His cigarette-end dropped beside his heel, and was trodden out. The blue eyes never looked down at it.

'You're right – the Saint has been something of a crook sometimes, even if that didn't hurt anybody but specimens like you. And since I reformed I've become rather sophisticated. Maybe it's a pity. One loses sight of some simple elementary things that were very good. It wasn't always like that. Since you know my name so well, you may remember that I once had only one cure for creatures like you. I was judge and executioner.'

The train thundered south, perfected machinery roaring on its unswerving lines through a world of logic and materialism forged into wheels. And in one compartment of it Bruce Voyson sat mute, clutched in an eerie spell that drove like a clammy wind through the logic on which he had based his life.

'Romantic, wasn't it?' went on that incredible voice. 'But the law has so many loopholes. Before it can hang you for murder you've got to beat your victim's brains out with a club. And yet you are a murderer, aren't you? Just a few minutes ago a friend of ours would have committed suicide on your account if I hadn't spotted him in the nick of time. For all I know, others may have done the same thing already. Certainly some of your victims will. And while that's going on, you're on your way to Batavia to enjoy at least two million dollars of their money – two millions which would do a little towards helping them to a fresh start. And all those dollars would be available for the receivers if you met with an unfortunate accident. There doesn't seem to be any obvious reason why you should go on living, does there?'

Simon Templar put his hand in his pocket and took out the folder of tickets. Deliberately he tore it across twice and scattered the pieces out of the window. Voyson started forward with a strangled gasp, and looked into the muzzle of his own gun.

'You've reminded me of days that I like to remember,' said the Saint. 'There is a justice above the law; and it seems just that a man like you should die.'

Voyson's red-rimmed eyes narrowed, and then he flung himself across the short space.

4

Simon took out a handkerchief and wiped the gun carefully all over. It was a small-calibre weapon, and the single crack of it should not have alarmed anyone who heard it among the other noises of the train.

Still holding it in his handkerchief, he folded Voyson's fingers around the butt, taking care to impress their prints on the shiny surface. Voyson slumped in the corner, with the bullet puncture in his right temple showing in the centre of a shaded circle of burnt cordite. Working with dispassionate speed, the Saint dropped his sandwich and pepper-pot out of the window, picked up a couple of crumbs, and erased his fingerprints from the handle. He wiped the inside catch of the door in the same way, slid it back, and brushed his handkerchief over the outside as he closed it again. There was no flaw in the scene; nothing could have seemed more natural than that a man in Voyson's position should have lost his nerve and taken the easy way out. Simon was without pity or regret.

But as he went back to his own compartment he felt happy. He had always known that the old days were good; and the return had its own emotion.

He saw his fellow-travellers again with a sense of surprise and unreality. For a while he had almost forgotten them. But the old German caught his hand as he sat down, holding it in a kind of tremulous eagerness, with a pathetic brilliance awake in his dulled eyes.

'I vant to thank you,' he said. 'You safe me from doing something very foolish. I vas a coward – a traitor. I run away.'

'Don't we all?' said the Saint.

The old man shook his head.

'Dot vould have been a wicked thing to do. But I am not like dot now. Perhaps it isn't so bad. I am used to vork, und at my age I have so much experience, I am a better vorkman than any young man. So I say I go back und vork again. Does a few more years matter so much?'

'And I'm going to work too,' said the girl. 'Between us, we'll get it all back twice as quickly.'

Simon looked at them both for a long time.

There were ninety thousand dollars in his pocket, which was money in any man's life. He could have enjoyed every cent of it. He didn't want to see what he was seeing.

And yet, half against his will, against the resentful primitive selfishness which is rooted in every man, adventurer or not, he found himself looking at something grand and indestructible. Even the enigma of the Rhine Maiden baffled him no longer. He saw it only as the riddle of the ultimate woman waiting for life in the fearless faith of the enchanted castle, waiting for the knight in shining armour who must come riding down the hills of the morning with her name on his shield. And he did not want to see the magic dimmed.

'I don't think you'll have to do that,' he said.

He smiled, and held out the thin folds of bills he had taken. Life was still rich; he could take plenty more. And some things were cheap at any price.

'I had a word with Voyson myself. I think I made him see that he couldn't get away with what he was doing. Anyway, he changed his mind. He asked me to give you this.'

The train was slowing up; and a guard came down the corridor shouting '*Hier Mainz, alles umsteigen!*' Simon stood up and took down his valise. Being human, he was aware that the girl's eyes were fixed on him with an odd breathlessness; and he thought that she could carry with her many worse ideals.

Tirol
The Golden Journey

INTRODUCTION BY LESLIE CHARTERIS*

... there are just a few stories which I genuinely regret losing,
which were lost by force of circumstance and which I can do
nothing about. They were all original Saint stories too, and I
was thinking of them while working on a new collection of
shorter pieces which I am now trying to finish up.

One of them, called 'The Golden Journey', was an open-
air story about hiking in Germany in 1931, which was
published in *Harper's* the following year. In 1931, if you
remember, the French had only just moved out of the
Rhineland, and Hitler was nothing but a beer-hall politician,
and there was a new spirit among the youth of Germany – a
spirit which at that time I think might have developed into
something very fine if Naziom hadn't taken it over and chan-
neled it in the way we know. In those days they spent all their
spare time rucksacking through the countryside of bicycles
or on foot, singing along the roads and singing at night in the
inns; it was, I thought at the time, a lot better than crashing
around in hot rods and jitterbugging, although we know what
it come to. It was a great background for a happy story then,
and yet it is a story which I think it may never be possible to
revive. Too many ugly things stand between that memory
and the present and they cannot be forgotten even a period
of peace. But the story depends on that background entirely
and can't be translated to any other time nor place. So, let it

*From *A Letter from the Saint* (1947)

die, along with many other pleasant things that will never
come back.

(Editorial note: Needless to say, it was revived ...)

I

Probably if Belinda Deane hadn't been born with such liquid brown eyes, such a small straight nose, such a delicious mouth, and such a delightful chin, she would never have been spoiled. And if she hadn't been spoiled, Simon Templar would never have felt called upon to interfere. And if he hadn't interfered . . . But the course of far more important histories has been changed by the curve of an eyebrow before now.

Belinda Deane knocked on the door of his hotel bedroom in Munich at half-past twelve, which was less than an hour after his breakfast; and he put down his razor and went cheerfully to let her in.

'I – I'm sorry,' she said, when she saw him.

'Why?' Simon asked. 'Don't you approve of this dressing-gown?'

He returned to the mirror and calmly resumed the scraping of his face. The girl stood with her back to the door, twisting a scrap of handkerchief in her fingers.

'Mr Templar,' she said, 'my bag's been stolen.'

'How did that happen?'

'I was in my room. I – I left it for a few minutes, and when I came back it was gone!'

'Too bad,' murmured the Saint gravely.

He turned the angle of his jawbone with care, stretching his head sideways. His unruffled accents held a sublime and seraphic Saintliness of innocence which in itself was a volume of explanation for his nickname. It took the girl's breath away for a moment; and then she froze over.

'Too bad,' she said coldly, 'is putting it mildly. It had all my money in it, and my letter of credit, and my passport – everything. I've never been in such a mess in my life. What am I going to do?'

'Have you told the hotel about it?'

'Of course. I've had managers and clerks and detectives prowling about my room for the last half-hour.'

Simon shrugged.

'It seems a pity you didn't go on to Garmisch yesterday with Jack.'

She gazed at him glacially; but his back was turned to her and he was imperturbably intent on his shave. A glacial gaze inevitably loses much of its effect when it has to be reflected by a mirror and the recipient is merely paying the polite minimum of attention anyhow. The disadvantage made her furious, and she controlled herself with an effort. Simon's amused blue eyes decided that Jack Easton had certainly picked a Tartar; but he admitted that wrath and hauteur sat very well on her small imperious face.

'If you remember,' she said with unnatural restraint, 'I told my fiancé that tramping about with him over a lot of dreary roads and sleeping in filthy village inns without any sanitation was not included in the terms of our engagement, and just wasn't my idea of a good time. I'm a civilized woman, not a farm hand. Also that happens to be my own business. Why don't you try to suggest something helpful?'

'You haven't any friends here?'

'None at all.'

The Saint raised one eyebrow.

'In that case, you're only left with your bank's correspondents here, or the American consulate. Failing those two,' he added flippantly, 'you could lie down on the tramlines outside and wait with resignation for the next tram—'

The door banged violently behind her; and Simon glanced at it and chuckled.

He ran cold water into the basin, submerged his head to remove the last traces of lather, and dried it off with a rough towel. Then he brushed his hair and sat down at the small desk where the telephone stood. He fished the directory out of a drawer, and with it the girl's expensive bag. From it he took her letter of credit, discovered the Munich correspondents named there, and called the number.

'This is the American consulate,' he said, when he was connected with the necessary Personage. 'We have information of a trick that's being played on the banks around here by an American girl. She comes in with the story that her letter of credit has been stolen, and tries to get an advance without it. There is no accurate description of her at the moment except that she is dark and about one metre sixty centimetres tall. Anything else we learn will be communicated to the police; but in the meanwhile we're taking the responsibility of warning the principal banks. Your safest course will be to make no advance in those circumstances. Tell the girl you will have to get in touch with New York or wherever it is, and ask her to call back in three or four days. By that time you'll have a full description from the police.'

A couple of minutes later he was speaking to the American consul.

'I say!' he bleated, in the plaintive tones of Oxford. 'D'you happen to know a young thing by the name of Deane – Miss Deane?'

'No,' said the consul blankly. 'What about her?'

'Well, I met her in a beer garden last night. She's an American girl – at least, she said she was. Dashed pretty, too. She told me her bag and things had been stolen, and I lent her five pounds to wire home for money. Well, I've just been sniffing a cocktail with another johnny and we were comparing notes, and it turns out he met the same girl in another beer garden last Tuesday and lent her ten dollars on the same story. So we toddled round to the hotel she said she was staying at to make inquiries, and they hadn't heard of her at all. So we decided she must be a crook, and we thought we'd better tell you to warn your other citizens about her, old boy!'

'I'm very much obliged. Can you tell me what she looks like?'

'Like a wicked man's dream, old fruit! About five foot three, with the most luscious brown eyes . . .'

His last call was to the hotel manager. Simon Templar spoke German, as he spoke other languages, like a native; and he put on his stiffest and most official staccato for the occasion.

'This is the Central Police Office. We have information received that a new swindle is by an American girl worked. She tells you that her money from her room in your hotel stolen is. Then will she a few days more to stay attempt, or money to borrow . . . So! That has already yourself befallen . . . No, unfortunately is there nothing to do. It is impossible the untruthfulness of her story to prove. You must however no compensation pay; and if you her room engaged announce, will you surely less money lose.'

Simon finished his dressing in an aura of silent laughter, and went out to lunch.

He was scanning a magazine in his room about four o'clock when another knock came on his door and the girl walked in. She looked pale and tired; but the Saint hardened his heart. Even the spectacle of his attire could only rouse her to a faint spark of sarcasm.

'Have you joined the boy scouts or something?' she asked.

Simon turned his eyes down to his brown knees unabashed.

'I'm going down to Innsbruck and up over the Brenner

pass into Italy. Tramping about over a lot of dreary roads and sleeping in ditches – all that sort of thing. It's one of the most beautiful trips in the whole world, and the only way you can get the best out of it is on foot. I'm catching a train to Lenggries at five, and starting from there early tomorrow morning – that cuts out the only dull part. What luck have you had?'

'None at all.' The girl flung herself into a chair. 'I'd never have believed anything could have been so hopeless. My God, the way I've been looked at today, you might think I was some kind of crook! I went to the bank. Yes, they'd be delighted to get in touch with my bank in Boston, but they couldn't do anything till they had a reply. How long would it take? Four days at least. And what was I going to do till then? The manager didn't know, but he shrugged his shoulders as if he thought I'd be lucky to stay out of jail that long. Then I went to the consulate. The consul's eyes were popping out of his head almost as soon as I'd begun to tell him the trouble. If the bank was willing to cable Boston for me, what was the trouble? I told him I couldn't go without eating for four days. He said he was only authorized to allow me fifty cents a day and send me home. I asked him what he thought I could eat for fifty cents, and he bawled me out! He said I was a disgrace to the country, and an American citizen had no business to be abroad without any means of support, and if he shipped me home I'd go straight to jail when I landed. And then he showed me the door. I've never been so humiliated in my life! If I don't get that consul fired out of the service—'

'But surely you can stay on here till some money arrives?' suggested the Saint ingenuously.

'Not a chance. I've just seen the manager. He said as much as he could without insulting me openly – told me he would require my room by seven o'clock if I couldn't pay him up to date by that time.'

'Distinctly awkward,' remarked Simon judicially.

The girl bit her lip.

'I – I've got to do something,' she stammered. 'I don't know how to say it – I hate asking you, after all this – but I've got to have something to see me through till the bank gets a reply from Boston, and they can't do that till after the week-end. Or when Jack gets to Innsbruck about Tuesday – I can send a wire to him there. I – I know I'm practically a stranger, but if you could lend me just enough—'

'My dear,' said the Saint bluntly, 'I should be delighted. But I haven't got it to lend.'

Her eyes opened wide.

'You haven't got it?'

He spread out a brown hand.

'Take a look. My luggage went off in advance this after-noon. All I'm going to need – toothbrush and towel and blan-kets – is in my rucksack. My bill here is paid, and I've got about forty marks in my belt – enough to buy food and beer. I can't get any more till I get to Bolzano. I couldn't even send you to Innsbruck – the third-class fare for one is about fifteen marks, and the remaining twenty-five wouldn't feed me.'

She stared at him aghast. Her pretty mouth quivered. There was a moistness very close to the tears of sheer hyster-ical fright in her eyes.

'But what on earth am I going to do?' she wailed.

Simon lighted a cigarette, and allowed his gaze to return to her face.

'You'll just have to walk to Innsbruck with me,' he said.

2

Simon Templar had been cordially disliked by many differ-ent people in his time, but rarely with such a wholehearted simplicity as that which Belinda Deane lavished on him the next morning. On the other hand, unpopularity had never lowered his spirits: he strode along carolling to the skies, and meditating on the infinite variety of the acci-dents of travel.

He had met Belinda Deane and Jack Easton on the train from Stuttgart a week before. There had been some compli-cation about their tickets, and their knowledge of German was infinitesimal. The Saint, to whom human companion-ship was the breath of life, and who would seize any excuse to beguile a journey by making the acquaintance of his fellow-travellers, had stepped in as an interpreter. Thereafter they had gone around Munich together, until Easton had separ-ated to join an old friend – 'a great-open-space friend', he described him – on a short walking trip from Garmisch to Innsbruck by way of Oberammergau. This decision had been the subject of a distressing scene at which Simon had been coerced into the position of umpire.

It was not by any means the first he had witnessed. One glance had been sufficient to tell him that Belinda had been blessed with a face and figure that would make even hard-boiled waiters scramble for the privilege of serving her; but one hour in her company had been enough to show him that they must have been doing it ever since she left her cradle, with the inevitable results. Everything that New England and Paris had to give had been endowed upon her – background, breed, education, poise. She could have been taken for the flower of American sophistication at its most perfect. Intelligence, knowledge, charm – she had them all. She knew exactly the right thing to say and do in any circumstances; entirely because she had been trained to circumstances where the same things were always being said and done. Jack Easton, a youngster of less ancient lineage, confessed that there were times when she scared him.

'Sometimes she ought to be spanked,' he said once, when he and Simon were alone together after that last scene.

He was annoyed, because the quarrel had consisted of a healthily stubborn bluntness piling up in competition with an increasingly chilly self-possession; and there was something about the Saint which always drew out confidences.

'What she really needs,' said Easton, 'is for somebody to club her and drag her off to a desert island and make her wash dishes and dig up her own potatoes.'

'Why don't you do it?' murmured the Saint.

'Because I know she'd never forgive me as long as she lived. Besides,' said Easton, morosely practical, 'I don't know any desert islands.'

Simon smoked for a time before he replied. The idea had come to him on the spur of the moment, and the more he thought of it the more it made him smile. The troubles of young love had always seemed more worth while to him than most things.

'It wouldn't matter so much if she never forgave me,' he had said. 'And it could be done without desert islands.'

Belinda trotted beside him and hated him. The leisurely swing of his long legs was measured to a pace that made her work to keep up with him. His pack rode like a feather on his broad shoulders, and the possibility of fatigue didn't seem to enter his head. She glanced sidelong at his strong brown profile, down over his check cotton shirt with rolled-up sleeves, his broad leather belt, leather shorts, and bare legs; and hated him still more for the ease of his untrammelled masculinity. She had been moved to sarcasm at the expense of his costume in the hotel; but now she tried not to admit that the curious glances of the few people they passed were centred on her. Her light tweed skirt came from Paris, her green suède golfing jacket was the latest thing from Fifth Avenue: from the rudimentary crown of her jaunty little hat to the welts of her green and white buckskin shoes she was as smart and pretty as a picture, and she knew it. It was unjust that that smartness should give her no advantage.

The Saint sang.

> *'Give me the life I love,*
> *Let the lave go by me—'*

Belinda gritted her small white teeth. She had never done much walking, and after the first few miles she was feeling tired. The fact that the man at her side should have been able to allot the major ration of his breath to singing was like a deliberate affront. She began to wonder for the first time why she should ever have considered his fantastic proposition; but it had seemed like the only practical solution. Even now, she could think of nothing else that she could have done. And from the moment when she had wearily accepted, he had taken charge – registered her luggage to Innsbruck, paid the carriage fees, rushed her to the station, almost abducted her while her mind was still numbed by the shock of inconceivable circumstances ... The morning grew hotter, and she struggled out of her jacket.

'Could you find room for this somewhere?' she asked, like a queen conferring a favour.

The Saint cocked a clear blue eye at her.

'Lady,' he said, 'this pack weighs twenty-five pounds. Are you sure you can't manage twelve ounces?'

She walked on speechlessly.

The scenery meant nothing to her. Roads were merely the links in an endless trail, which ended tantalizingly at every bend and the crest of every rise, only to lead on again immediately. When he called the first halt, at the end of nearly four hours' marching, she fell on the dusty grass by the roadside and wondered if she would ever be able to get up again.

'My stockings have holes in them,' she said.

He nodded.

'There's nothing like plenty of ventilation to keep your feet in condition.'

She tore off her stockings without a word and threw them away; but her hands trembled. Simon, unmoved, opened his pack and produced food – coarse black bread and butter, cheese, and liver sausage.

'How about some lunch?'

She looked at the bread down her nose.

'What's that stuff?'

'The most wholesome bread in the world. All the vitamins, minerals and roughage that any dietitian could desire. Preserves the teeth and massages the intestines.'

'I don't care for it, thank you.' As a matter of fact, she was at the stage where her stomach felt too tired for food. 'All I want is a drink.'

'We'll stop at the next village and get some beer.'

'I don't drink beer.'

The Saint ploughed appreciatively on into his massive hunk of bread.

'The water should be all right in that stream over there,' he said, indicating it with a movement of his hand.

'Are you suggesting,' she inquired icily, 'that I should get down on all fours and lap it up like a cow?'

Simon chewed.

'Like a gazelle,' he said, 'would be more poetic.'

She closed her eyes and lay there motionlessly; and if he sensed the simmering of the volcano he gave no sign of it. He ate his fill and smoked a cigarette; then he walked over to the stream, drank frugally, and bathed his face. When he came back she was sitting up. He strapped his pack and hoisted it deftly.

'Ready?'

Somehow she picked herself up. Her muscles had stiffened during the rest, and it was agony to squeeze her feet back into her shoes, which were cut for appearance rather than comfort. Only a strained and crackling obstinacy drew the effort out of her: the mockery of his cool blue gaze told her only too frankly that he was waiting for her to break down, and she wondered how long she would be able to cheat him of that satisfaction.

He drove her on relentlessly. Hills rose and fell away. Scattered cottages, tilled fields, pastures, woods, blurred by in a crawling panorama. They marched through a deep forest of mighty trees where wood-cutters were working, along a road lined with stacks of brown logs. The sweet-smelling air held the music of whining saws and the clunk and ring of axes; but it meant nothing to her but an interval of blessed relief from the heat of the sun. Even then, the shadowy vastness of it was a little terrifying. She had never been so close to the rich mightiness of the earth: to her 'country' had only been something rather cute and amusing, a drawing-room picture brought into three dimensions, to be visited as a stunt in the company of sleek automobiles whose purring mechanism drowned the silences with their reassurance of civilized man's conquest of nature. Without that comfort she was like a child left in the dark. On the rare occasions when a car passed them she watched it yearningly, and then licked the dust from her lips and felt lonelier when it had gone. Once a cart kept them company for a quarter of an hour, while Simon and the driver exchanged shouted witticisms.

Presently their path led beside a small river, with a tall ledge of rock rising on their left. The going was worse there, strewn with loose stones which seemed to slip backwards with her as fast as she went forward. The crunch of them under her plodding footsteps resolved itself into a maddening rhythm of hate. '*Beast – bully – swine – beast – bully – swine!*' they drummed out, bruising her feet at every step. Then she slipped on one. There was a tearing sound, and she stopped and leaned against the rocky wall.

'My heel's come off.'

'What's holding your toes on?' asked the Saint interestedly.

Suddenly all her pent-up bitterness boiled over, so that for a moment she forgot her weariness. Her eyes blazed, and his tanned features swam in her vision. Before she knew what she was doing she had smacked his face.

When her sight cleared again he had not moved.

'Belinda,' he said quietly, 'there's another lesson you obviously haven't learned. When a girl strikes a man she's trading on a false idea of chivalry. If you do that again I shall put you across my knee.'

'You wouldn't dare!' she panted; but for the first time in her life she was afraid.

He made no attempt to argue with her. Lowering his pack, he opened it and took out a pair of plain leather sandals.

'I thought something like that would happen. These are your size, and you'll find them much more comfortable.'

He waited while she took off her shoes and threw them into the river, where they floated forlornly like derelict emblems of respectability. Looking down at her feet, she felt the incongruity of her attire and jerked off the jaunty little hat. Shortly afterwards she lost patience with carrying it and let it fall by the wayside – another relic of herself to be marked up in the score of hatred which was etched on her soul in burning acid.

Evening found their path widening out into a bowl of open land, flat and stony, where the river diverged into a network of rambling channels winding and intersecting across an area of hard barren ground broken by a few stunted trees and clumps of parched grass. Simon pointed to a house that was visible on a slight rise in the midst of it.

'That's an inn,' he said, 'and there will be beer.'

She saw it as a prospect of rest, a thousand leagues distant. She was so tired that each individual step called for a separate effort, and she had to keep her eyes fixed on the objective to force herself to complete the distance. The guest-room inside was unlighted and gloomy: she expected it was filthy as well, but she was past caring. She sank on to a wooden bench, put her elbows on the stained bare table, and buried her face in her hands.

By that time there was a gnawing void of hunger below her ribs; and when the serving-girl came she ordered chocolate. Simon called for beer, with an extra tankard for the game-keeper who sat puffing his pipe in the far corner.

The gamekeeper was a big slow-spoken man with a lined weather-beaten face like a walnut. He wore the costume of the country – small green felt hat with a brush at the back, leather shorts hung on embroidered leather suspenders, striped woollen gaiters which left his ankles bare. Simon steered him to the subject of camping. The gamekeeper said it was forbidden in the woods on the east, through which a footpath would take them across the frontier into Austria. It was a great pity, said the gamekeeper, because he knew what would have been an ideal spot only a few hundred metres away; and he winked prodigiously, and roared with laughter. Simon bought him another tankard of beer, and they brought the serving-girl into the conversation. The low-ceilinged room rang with the ebb-and-flow of their carefree voices.

Belinda drank her hot syrupy chocolate, and thought: 'He's vulgar, he's common, he only wants to humiliate me. How could he have anything to talk about with people like that? He can come in here and flirt with a little servant-girl like a tough in a saloon. That man must despise him. It's horrible! Oh, my God, why didn't I know what he was like before?' She couldn't understand a word, and nobody paid any attention to her. She had never been ignored before. 'They're all cheap, all of them,' she thought. 'They don't talk to me because they know I belong to a different class.' She raised her chin and tried to express this superiority in her attitude; but it was cold comfort. When Simon returned to her it was almost a relief.

'I'd like to have something to eat and go straight to bed,' she said.

The Saint raised his eyebrows.

'You can have some food as soon as we're settled in; but we aren't settling in here.'

'I tell you I can't walk another yard,' she said haggardly. 'Can't you see I'm half dead?'

'I'm afraid you'll have to walk another three hundred yards or so.'

'What's wrong with this place?'

He gestured with his tankard.

'We're sleeping in the woods.'

She stared at him incredulously.

'I don't understand you.'

'In the woods,' explained the Saint. *Im wald. Dans le bois. Unter den Linten.*'

'You must be crazy.'

'Not at all. The partridges do it, and suffer no grievous harm. I've done it often enough myself, and very rarely died of it. You don't seem to understand the situation. Ambling along as we are, it'll take us about a week to get to Innsbruck. At the moment, we are the proud possessors of some thirty-five marks. You pay four marks for a bed in a Gasthaus; and we've still got to eat.'

She realized that the man in the corner was watching her curiously. It came to her that at all costs her dignity must leave that room untouched. The inexorable mathematics of Simon's argument scarcely made any impression on her; she was in the grip of circumstances that were crushing her till she could have screamed, but she could not make a scene and bring herself down to the level she had just despised.

She stood up and went out without speaking, Simon following her. It had grown darker; and the twitter and chirp and rustle of night creatures was all around them as they entered the wood. Simon took the lead, humming. The spot the gamekeeper had described was near a tributary of the river they had recently quitted, a grassy hollow away from the footpath and a few feet above the stream. Simon's expert eye appraised it and found no fault. He lowered his pack to the ground and began to unfasten it.

'Will you get some water while I make the fire?' he said.

He put the billycan down beside her, and went off to gather dry logs. In a very short time he had kindled a cheerful blaze: and she huddled gratefully up to it, for it had turned colder after the sun went down. Simon took bread, eggs, and butter from his rucksack, and picked up the billy. It was empty.

'I asked you to get some water,' he said.

She raised her sullen eyes to him over the fire.

'I'm not a servant,' she said.

'Neither am I,' said the Saint quietly. 'You'll do your share or go hungry – whichever you prefer.'

The girl struggled to her feet.

'Oh, I could kill you!' she cried passionately, and went groping down to the stream.

3

Belinda fell asleep at first out of pure exhaustion; but it was still dark when she woke up again. The fire had died down to a cone of red embers, and there was a chill in the air that made her shiver. She pulled the spare width of her groundsheet over her, as Simon had shown her how to do if it began to rain; but it was too thin to give any warmth. Even a summer night turns cool out of doors towards two and three o'clock: unsuspected little breezes stir the air and strike through the thickest blankets The body's warmth, unguarded by the moderating vigilance of walls and ceilings, drifts away like smoke in the limitless vastness of space.

The grass, which had looked so flat and felt so soft, developed innumerable bumps and hardnesses which bruised her bones. A tenuous dampness rose from it; and when she moved her head on the unsympathetic pillow of her sandals rolled up in a towel it felt wet and cold. The star-sprinkled sky, lofting billions of empty miles over her head, panicked her with its aloofness from her own microscopic insignificance. Oh, blessed civilization and the flattering barricades of pigmy architecture, which has made us afraid of the supernal majesty of our first home! . . . The woods around her were full of moving shadows and the whisper of tiny scuttering feet, the flutter of a miniature cosmos hunting and fighting and dying and marching on. The throbbing wings of an owl passing overhead made her heart leap into her mouth . . .

She lay there aching and fearful, waiting and praying for

the sky to pale with the dawn, hating and yet glad of the company of the man who slept peacefully on the other side of the fire. She dozed and woke again, stiff and cold and miserable. Untold ages passed before the roof of the world lightened; other countless æons went by before the first beams of the sun gilded the topmost leaves of the trees. When the rays reached her they might give her a little warmth, and she would be able to sleep again. A flock of birds whirred cheeping across the faded stars. The golden radiance on the tree-tops crept down with maddening slowness . . .

When her eyes opened again it was broad daylight. The fire had been coaxed to life again. It crackled and hissed cheerily, while Simon Templar bent over it on one knee and juggled with the billy and a sizzling frying-pan.

'Eight o'clock and a lovely morning, Belinda,' he said.

The fragrance of boiling coffee came to her nostrils, and she felt half sick with hunger and sleeplessness. She pulled herself up, instinctively searching for comb and mirror; and what she saw in the glass horrified her.

'I must get a wash,' she said.

He passed her a cake of soap.

'The bath's right on the doorstep, and breakfast will be ready in five minutes.'

The cold water nipped her face and hands, but it freshened her. Afterwards she dealt ravenously with scrambled eggs and two slices of the coarse black bread, and smoked a cigarette with her coffee. When it was done, the Saint climbed to his feet and stretched himself.

'I'll make the beds,' he said. 'It's your turn to wash up.'

She looked resentfully at the pan, slimy with the congealed yellowness of egg, and shuddered.

'How do you expect me to do that?' she asked dangerously.

'It's easy enough. I'll show you.'

He led the way down the bank to the edge of the stream.

He scooped a handful of earth into the pan, plucked up a tuft of grass by the roots, and held the two things out to her.

'Scrub the earth around with the grass, and repeat until clean. Rinse and dry.'

All her hatred and disgust was seething up again, but she tried to keep her balance. To lose her temper was the worst way to go about undermining his insolent assurance.

'There are limits,' she said, as evenly as she could, 'and I think you've reached them.'

'Hadn't it occurred to you that dishes have to be washed?'

'It hadn't occurred to me that a man could ask me to put my hands into a foul mess like that. But perhaps I still thought you might have some of the more elementary instincts of a gentleman. It was rather an absurd mistake to make, wasn't it?'

'Very,' said the Saint carefully. 'Especially after last night. As I explained to you – camp chores are split two ways. Can you make a fire?'

'I've never tried.'

'Then it's safe to assume you can't. Can you cook?'

'Unfortunately I wasn't brought up in a kitchen.'

'In that case you can only make yourself useful by fetching water and washing up. If you like eating scrambled eggs, you can help by cleaning up after them. If you don't like that, you can live on bread and water, which involves no washing. The diet is dull, but you won't starve on it. Let's have it quite clear. You chose to travel this way—'

'I've never regretted anything so much in my life.'

'You might have regretted being locked up in a German prison still more. I'm not running a conducted tour with a team of cooks and bottle-washers trailing behind. This is a simple matter of the fair division of labour. There are six more days of it coming, and you may as well try to get through them decently.'

'What do you think I am?' she flared. 'A working slut like that girl at the inn?'

His eyes met hers steadily.

'I think you're an idle loafer who ought to learn a little about honest work. I think you've lain so soft all your life that you need some hardship and crude discomfort to catch your spine before it dissolves altogether. Both those things are going to happen to you before we get to Innsbruck. You've ceased to be ornamental; so now you're going to turn into a useful working squaw – and like it!'

'Am I?' she said; and then her open hand struck him across the face.

It was done before she knew what she was doing, an instant after she had knocked the pan spinning out of his light grasp into mid-stream, her thin and ragged self-control bursting like tissue before the intolerable flame of her resentment. The torrent of words came afterwards: she saw him smile quietly, and lashed out in sudden fear at the good-humoured white flash of his teeth, but her clenched fist met empty air.

He bent her over his knee and did exactly what he had promised to do, with an impersonal efficiency quite devoid of heat. When he released her she was sobbing with impotent rage and real stinging pain. She turned and ran blindly up the bank: if she had had a knife she would have driven it into his throat, but without it her one idea was to get away. Half unconsciously she found the path which he had pointed out as the one that ran into Austria. There must be a road somewhere farther on: there would be cars, someone would give her a lift. Her eyes were wet and swimming with shame and anger.

Then she looked back and saw him following her. She glimpsed his tall figure through the trees, rucksack on back, swinging lithely along without making any effort to overtake her. She plunged on till her lungs were bursting and the agony of her stiffened joints made every step a torture; but he was always the same distance behind, unhurried and inescapable as doom. She had to rest or fall down. 'Go away! Go away!' she cried, and struggled on with her heart pounding.

The trees thinned out, and she saw telegraph poles on the other side of a field. She ran out into the road. A truck was coming towards her, headed south: she stood in the middle of the road and waved to it till it stopped.

'Take me wherever you're going!' she babbled. 'Take me to Innsbruck! I'll pay you anything you ask!'

The driver looked down at her uncomprehendingly.

'Innsbruck?' He pointed down the road. '*Dorthin; aber es ist sehr weit zu laufen—*'

She pantomimed frantically, trying to make him understand. Why couldn't she speak German? . . . and then the Saint's clear voice spoke coolly from the side of the road, in the driver's own idiom.

'Permit me to introduce my wife. A little family argument. Please don't bother. She'll get over it.'

The driver's mouth and eyes opened in an elaborate '*Ach, so!*' of intelligence, the bottomless sympathy of one woman-ridden male to another. He chuckled, and engaged his gears.

'*Verzeihen Sie, mein Herr! Ich habe auch eine Frau!*' he flung backwards as he drove on.

Belinda's strength drained out of her. She threw herself down at the side of the road and wept, with her face hidden in her arms. The Saint's quiet voice spoke from above her head like the voice of destiny.

'It's no good, Belinda. You can't run away. Life has caught up with you.'

Days followed through which she moved in a kind of fog – days of physical exhaustion, dark rooms in inns, meals tastelessly yet ravenously devoured, washing of dishes and ruin of manicured hands, lumpy beds on the bare ground, scorching sun, dust, sweat, rain and cold. Once, after a day of ceaseless drizzle, when she had to sleep in her sodden clothes on earth that squelched under the flimsy groundsheet, she was certain she must catch pneumonia and die, and felt cruelly injured when the fresh air and healthy life refused even to let her catch a cold in the nose. She had those moods of self-pity when any added affliction would have been welcome, so that she could have looked up to Heaven like Job and protested that no one had ever suffered so much. Self-pity alternated with the hours when her mind was filled with nothing but murderous hatred of the man who was always beside her, calm and unchanging as a mountain, blithely unruffled in good weather and bad. She carried out the tasks he set her because she had no choice; but she swore she would die before he could say he had broken her spirit. At first she washed the frying-pan perfunctorily, and brought it back with scraps of earth still clinging to the stubborn traces of egg: he said nothing about it, but that night he scrambled only two eggs and gave them to her, grey and gritty with the remains of mud she had left.

'That's your ration,' he said remorselessly. 'If you don't like it, have the pan clean next time.'

Next time she finished her scouring with the towel, and when she wanted to wash she tried to take his. He stopped her.

'Egg is grand for the complexion,' he said. 'But if you object to drying your face on a dishcloth, the usual remedy applies – plus washing the towel.'

Sometimes she thought she would steal his knife while he slept and cut his throat: the impulse was there, but she knew she would have been lost without him. Even when the rain had poured all day and everything was drenched, he conjured dry wood out of empty air and had a fire going in no time; he introduced unexpected variety into their simple fare, and robbed orchards for apples with the abandoned enthusiasm of a school-boy. He was never bad-tempered or at a loss: he smoothed difficulties away without appearing to notice them. For thirty-six hours after her spanking she sulked furiously, but it made no mark on his tranquillity. The tension of laboured silence slipped perforce into a minimum of essential conversation – strained and hostile on her part, unfailingly natural and good-humoured on his. Three days passed before she discovered that his eyes were soundlessly laughing at her.

Nothing is more difficult than for two people to be together every hour of the day and punctiliously ignore each other's existence. Nothing, she found out miserably, can grow more irksome than keeping alive a grudge against the someone who is utterly untroubled by rancour. Sometimes the loneliness of her self-imposed silence welled up on her so that she could have shrieked aloud for relief. Imperceptibly, the minimum of essential remarks seemed to increase. Every detail of their daily life became an excuse for some trivial speech which it was torment to resist. She found herself chattering for a quarter of an hour about the pros and cons of boiled and fried onions.

And then came the incredible night when she slept straight through until morning, and woke up contented. For a while the feeling baffled her, and she lay on her back and puzzled about it.

And then it dawned on her in a surprising flash. She was no longer tired! They had covered twenty miles the previous day, by the Saint's reckoning, and yet her limbs felt supple and relaxed, and her feet were not sore. Had they chosen an exceptionally soft piece of ground in which to camp, or had her body learned to adapt itself to the unyielding couch as well as to the abrupt changes from heat to cold? She could not understand it, but the night lay behind her as an interval of unbroken rest, blissful as a child's or a wild animal's. The consciousness of her surroundings came to her with a sense of shock. They had rolled into their blankets high up on a wooded slope on the southern shores of the Achensee: from where she lay she could see fragments of the placid waters of the lake gleaming like splinters of pale blue grass between the trees. On her left, the woods curved up and away in a rich green rolling train to the mighty shoulders of a white-capped peak that took the morning light to its brow in glistening magnificence. When she looked directly upwards, nothing came between her gaze and the arching tent of the sky where three fluffy white clouds floated slowly eastwards with the red glow of the recent sunrise catching them like the reflection of a fire. She had never really seen a sky before, or the glory of trees and rolling hills.

Belinda drank in a picture of unimagined beauty whose very strangeness made it unforgettable. In truth it was nothing scenically startling, not in any way the kind of view to which tourist excursions are run; it was only an odd corner of the natural splendour of the world, all of which is beautiful. But it was the first corner of the world to which her eyes had ever been opened with emotion, a starting point of undreamed-of experience which must be for ever as unique as all beginnings. Dazed with it as if she had awakened on a different planet, she climbed out of her blankets at last and searched mechanically for comb and mirror. The reflection that met her eyes seemed like the portrait of a stranger. Wind and sun had tinted a delicate gold into her skin, and there was a soft flush in her cheeks that had never been there before unless she dabbed it on. Her lips were riper, her eyes clearer and brighter than she had ever thought Nature could make them. She was entranced with herself.

She put her bare feet on the grass, and the sweet touch of the dew on them made the rest of her body aware of being soiled and sticky. Reluctant to separate her toes from the green coolness, and yet eager to perfect that physical joyousness in every way, she strapped on her sandals. In the days before that, she realized with amazement, she had been too weary, too numb with self-pity, to care about anything but superficial cleanliness.

She dug out the soap and went down to the lake shore, carrying her towel. What a perfume there was in the chill of the air, what a friendly peace in the stillness of earth and sky! She stood on the road by the shore and looked to her left towards the sleeping white houses of Pertisau, the specks of gaudily striped parasols on the lakeside terraces; and it was like looking at the vanguard of an invasion, and she was a savage come down from the clean hills to gaze in wonder at this outpost of civilization.

She stripped off her clothes and washed, and swam out a little way into the crystal water. It was very cold, but when she had dried herself she was tingling. She went up the hill again slowly, filled with an extraordinary happiness. She had no more envy of those people who were sleeping in soft beds half a mile away, who would presently rise and straggle down to eat their breakfasts in stuffy dining-rooms. How much they were missing – how much she had missed!

Breakfast . . . She was hungry, in a clear keen way that matched the air. She delved into the Saint's pack for food, picked up the frying-pan and inspected it. The fire was out, and when she turned over the heap of fuel beside it the wood was damp. How did one kindle a fire?

Simon Templar rolled over and opened his eyes. He hitched himself up on one elbow.

'Hullo – am I late?' he said, and glanced at his watch. It was half past six.

Belinda saw him with a start. She had forgotten . . . she hated him, didn't she? She remembered that she was still holding the frying-pan and dropped it guiltily.

'It's about breakfast-time,' she said. Her mouth felt clumsy. Odd, how hard it had become to make every word as impersonal and distant as she had trained herself to do – to convey with every sentence that she only spoke to him because she had to.

He threw off his blankets, and dived back into them again to return with two handfuls of twigs.

'Always sleep with some firewood and keep it dry,' he explained.

In a few seconds flames were licking up among the dead ashes, steaming the moisture from the other wood as he built it up around his tinder in a neat cone. He gathered the eggs together, and one of them escaped from his corral and went rolling down the hill. He ran after it, grabbed for it, and caught his toe on the projecting root of a tree: the chase ended in a headlong plunge and a complete somersault which brought him up with his back to the bole of a young sapling. There was something so comical about him as he sat there, with the rescued ovum triumphantly clutched in one hand, that Belinda felt a smile tugging at her lips. She fought against it; her chest ached, and the laughter tore at her throat; she gave way because she had to laugh or suffocate, and bowed before the gale. Simon was laughing too. The wall, the precious barrier that she had built up, was crumbling like sand in that tempest of mirth; and she could do nothing to hold it together . . .

Presently she was saying: 'Why don't you show me how to do those eggs; then I could take a turn with them?'

'It's easy enough when you know how. Like everything else, there's a trick in it. You've got to remember that a scrambled egg goes on cooking itself after you take it off the fire, so if you try to finish them in the pan they're hard and crumby when you serve them. Take them off while they still look half raw, and they end up just fine and juicy.'

She had never enjoyed a meal more in her life; and when it was finished she could not bear to think that they must leave that place at once. It was like a reprieve when he announced that his shirt was unspeakable, and they must pause for a washing day. They scrubbed their clothes in pools formed by the tiny waterfall that cascaded close by their camping-ground, and spread them in the sun to dry. It was mid-afternoon before she had to tear herself away: she went down with him to the road feeling newly refreshed and fit for a hundred miles before sundown, yet with the knowledge that she left part of her heart behind up there with the trees and sky.

As they reached the road a band of twenty young people were coming towards them, singing as they came. The men wore leather shorts and white linen shirts; some of the girls wore the same, others wore brief leather skirts. All of them carried packs, and many of the packs were heavy. Belinda saw one man laden with an enormous iron pot and a collection of smoke-blackened pans: he looked like a huge metallized snail.

'*Gruss Gott!*' cried the leader, breaking the song as he came up with them, in the universal greeting of Tyrolese wayfarers; and Simon smiled and answered '*Gruss Gott!*' The others of the party joined in. A couple from the middle fell out and stopped.

'*Wohin gehen Sie?*' asked the boy – he was little more. Simon told him they were on their way to Jenbach and thence to Innsbruck. 'We go also to Jenbach,' said the boy. '*Kommen Sie mit!*'

The group re-formed around them, and they went on together, past Seespitz and down the long hill that leads to the Inn valley. Belinda was happy. She was proud to be able to keep up with them tirelessly, and their singing made light of the miles. She was seeing everything as if she had been blind from her birth until that day. At one place a gang of men were working on the road; once she would have passed by without looking at them – they would have been merely common workmen, dirty but necessary cattle to serve the needs of those whose cars used the road. Now she saw them. They were stripped to the waist, bodies muscled like statues and polished with sweat like oil, harmonies of brown skin and blue cotton trousers. One party called '*Gruss Gott!*' to the other, smiling, fellow freeman of the air.

'What does that mean – *Gruss Gott?*' she asked the Saint.

'Greet God,' he answered, and looked at her. 'Isn't that only gratitude?'

The boy on her other side spoke a little English. She asked him where they came from and what they were doing.

'We are *Wandervogel*. We are tired of the cities, and we make ourselves gipsies. We sing for money, and work in the fields when we can, and make things to sell. Your sandals – they are a pattern made by the *Wandervogel*. We live now, and some day perhaps we die.'

'Are you happy?' she asked; and he looked at her in simple wonder.

'Why not? We do not want to be rich. We have all the world to live in, and we are free like the birds.'

They came to Jenbach in the cool of the evening; and again there was an inn. But this time it was different.

'We do not go with you any more,' said the boy. 'We go to Salzburg. But first we drink to our friendship.'

Belinda sat on a wooden bench and recalled the first time she had entered an inn. Then she had been too sick at heart to care whether it was dirty; now she would not have cared for a different reason, though she had learned that the inns were as clean as any room in her own home. Again there was a sunburned labourer sitting in the corner she chose, and the Saint talked with him, and when the serving-girl had distributed a tray-load of tankards she joined them and was chaffed and flirted with. It was the first Gasthof over again; the difference was in Belinda herself. Now she sat alert, eyes sparkling and shifting from one face to another in an attempt to follow the weaving shuttle of their voices; and when they laughed she laughed, pretending she understood. And the background of it all she did understand, without knowing how. There was a community of happiness and contentment, a fellowship and a freemasonry of people whose feet were rooted in the same good earth, a shared and implicit enjoyment of the food and drink and changing seasons, a spontaneous hospitality without self-consciousness, a unity of pagans who had greeted God. Man spoke to man, laughed, jested, holding back none of himself, untroubled by fears and jealousies: having no reason to do otherwise, each took the other immediately for a passing friend. Why not? The world they knew was large enough for them all. Why should not nation and nation meet in the same humanity? And Belinda found she was thinking too much; and she was glad when one man who had carried a mandolin slung across his back took it down and strummed a chord on the wires, and the voices round him rose in unison:

> *'Trink, trink, Bruderlein, trink,*
> *Lass doch die Sorgen zu Hause—'*

with the others chiming in, beating the tables with their tankards, till they were all singing—

> *'Meide den Kummer und meide den Schmerz,*
> *Dann ist das Leben ein Scherz;*

and the repetition rattled the glass in the windows:

'MEIDE DEN KUMMER UND MEIDE DEN SCHMERZ,
DANN IST DAS LEBEN EIN SCHERZ!'

Belinda listened; and Hilaire Belloc's lines, memorized parrot-fashion at school, went through her mind with a new haunting meaning: '*Do you remember an inn, Miranda, do you remember an inn?*' . . . That was an inn which she would always remember; and she felt strangely humble when the last strong hand had been shaken and she stood outside alone with Simon Templar under the darkening sky.

'How far is it from here to Innsbruck?' she asked as they walked away from the valley in search of a place to sleep.

'We could do it in one long day by the road, which is rather dull and dusty. Or if we struck out the way we're going, making a detour, it'd be two easy days.'

They were following a lonely cart-track, and every scuff of their footsteps sounded as clearly as if they had been alone in the world. A wagon laden with cordwood creaked out of the blue haze, drawn by a horse and a bullock in double harness; the wagoner cracked his whip and bade them good-evening as he went by. Was that a symbol of something? . . . Belinda said: 'Those *Wandervogel* must be very happy.'

'They belong to a new generation,' said the Saint quietly. 'There are many people like them here, under different names. It's an attempt to find a way out of the mess this world is in. The cities have failed them, and they're looking back to the ancient wisdom of contentment with simple things. At least it's better than idle hopelessness. And who's to say, maybe they've got something.' He looked around him. 'Here's grass, and a stream and wood to make a fire – shall we make this our camp?'

4

They cooked their food and ate in silence; but it was not the same silence as others that there had been. Belinda was oddly subdued; and Simon knew that his work was done. Afterwards, when it was finished and they sat on over cigarettes and enamel mugs of coffee, they were still quiet. Simon was thinking of other evenings of great peace in his life, as a man does in times of perfect contentment for the joy of comparing the incomparable; and he thought also of another more perilous adventure which had once taken him over the trail they had retraced. Belinda hugged her knees and gazed into the dancing flames. Why had she never noticed the sweet smell of wood-smoke before? . . . A log rolled over, scattering a small Vesuvius of sparks; and she said; 'What are things like where you're going after Innsbruck?'

Simon kicked the log back.

'They're better than anything you've seen yet. I don't think I've ever seen anything more beautiful in the world. It's a little bit like what we saw yesterday and today, only a hundred times more magnificent. Mountains and valleys and woods and streams. You take a trail that runs half-way up the wall of the world. On one side you can look up through the pines to the snow; on the other side you look down into a green valley with cattle grazing and a torrent racing at the bottom. The air's full of the scent of wild flowers and the tinkle of cow-bells. When you first come to it you feel you must just sit and look at it all day, taking it into your soul.'

Belinda listened to the murmur of insects in the grass, and everything she had seen that day passed before her in a pageant. At the end she saw the picture that Simon had painted for her. Young men and girls, sun-bronzed and care-free, swung along that trail half-way up the wall of the world, singing. They ate and slept and were happy around camp-fires like this. What a lot of useless desires we clutter up our lives with, she thought, and never know how unimportant they were until they have been almost forgotten!

What a mess of stupid formulas and trivialities! She lay on her back and stared up into the overarching fretwork of leaves. There was still something else to be said: it hurt her, but a new pride demanded it.

'I'm sorry I slapped you and wasted so many days,' she said. 'I'd give anything in the world to have them over again.'

He smiled in the firelight.

'I'll apologize for saying you'd ceased to be ornamental. It wasn't true, of course; but I wanted to make you mad. There was only a week, and we had to get the quarrelling over and done with. As a matter of fact, you're more decorative than you ever were before.'

He was so calm, so natural, that the effort of self-abase-ment which might have been a wound in her new peace of mind became nothing at all in retrospect. For that moment his unimpassioned understanding and wisdom seemed so godlike that she felt small – not uncomfortably and shame-facedly, but like a child.

'You've done so much for me,' she said, 'and yet I know nothing about you.'

He laughed.

'I'm just a rogue and a vagabond. Sometimes I'm enjoying a rest like this, sometimes I'm in much worse trouble. You'd only know me from my unlawful exploits, if you read about things like that. I throw my weight about and have no end of fun. Sometimes I steal.' He turned his blue eyes on her, and they danced. 'I stole your bag in Munich.'

She was too astounded even to gasp.

'You stole my bag?'

'Money and passport and letter of credit and everything. They're at the bottom of my pack now. And I spread some gorgeous rumours about you to the bank and the hotel and the consulate, so that you wouldn't be able to get any help – which explains why they were so nasty and suspicious. It was the only way I could get you in such a jam that you'd simply have to make this trip with me.'

She made no reply for a while; and then she said: 'Why should you take so much trouble over anyone like I was?'

'It was hardly any trouble to me,' he said, 'and I thought you were worth it. The way you were going, you were all set to make Jack thoroughly unhappy and break up both your lives. Jack said you'd never forgive him if he tried to get tough with you, but I figured it wouldn't do either of you so much harm if you never forgave me. All the same, I'm rather glad you have.'

Belinda bit her lip.

She was quiet again, very quiet, until they rolled into their blankets and went to sleep; and Simon let her be. Two more days, she told herself when she awoke; but the time went flying. One more night and a day – a day – three hours – two! . . . Everything she saw printed itself on her mind with the feeling that she was leaving it for ever. A boy driving a herd of cattle, slim, blond-haired, with transparent blue eyes and a merry smile. A castle built on a steep hill, hanging aloft in a solid curtain of pines like a picture nailed to a wall. The crucified Christs set up by every path and roadside and in many fields, with bunches of wild flowers stuck in the crevices of the carving – 'They're thank-offerings,' said the Saint. 'People going by put the flowers on them for luck.' Belinda

picked a handful of narcissi and arranged them behind the
outstretched arms of one figure; it seemed a pleasant thing to
do. She would never pass that way again, and she must
remember everything before she was outlawed from her
strange paradise . . . And then the last hour, and the inn at
Hall; where Simon left her on some pretext, and telephoned
a message to the address in Innsbruck which Jack Easton had
given him. Good-bye, good-bye! And she saw Innsbruck and
the end of the journey with a pang. It was so short, like a little
life which had to be laid down at its peak.

And then, somehow, relentlessly jarred out of the dream
into a cold light of commonplace, she was sitting in a beer
garden in Innsbruck with Jack Easton patting her hand.

'I was wrong, too, Belinda,' he was saying. 'This great open
space stuff isn't all it's cracked up to be. One day we were
being broiled alive, and the next it was pouring with rain and
we were soaked. God, and those country inns! Always the
same food, and sanitary arrangements straight out of the
Stone Age . . .'

She scarcely heard him at first. It was as if he spoke a
foreign language. She was looking up at the mountains that
girdle the town, which can be seen from every corner, loom-
ing above the house-tops like the bastions of a gigantic
fortress, the gates of the trail that ran half-way up the wall of
the world.

'Jack, I was the only one who was wrong. But we're going
on with Simon just like this, over the Alps into Italy.'

Easton shook his head.

'Nothing doing,' he stated firmly. 'I've had my share, and I
could do with some hot baths and civilized meals for a
change. We'll rent an automobile and drive over, if you like.'

Unbelieving, she stared at him. She had never seen him
before. Clean, carefully and inconspicuously dressed,
smoothly pink-faced, the embryo of a stolid pillar of the

civilized state. She looked down at herself, travel-stained and not caring. At the people around – townspeople mostly, sprinkled with tourists. They were like utter strangers; she looked at them with a queer pride, a pride in the dust and stains of the road that had become part of her, in which they had no part. She looked at Simon Templar, brown and dusty and strong like herself, sitting there with an amazed and motionless foreboding in his eyes. *He* was real. He belonged. Belonged back there under the wide reaches of the sky that she had once thought so terrible and comfortless, which now was the only ceiling of peace.

'Darling, your nose is peeling,' said Jack Easton jovially; and something that had been in her, which had grown dim and vague in the passing of seven days, was suddenly lifeless, dying without pain.

'No, no, no!' she cried, with her heart aching and awake. 'Simon, I can't go back. I can never go back!'

Lucerne
The Loaded Tourist

I

The lights of Lucerne were twinkling on the lakes as Simon
Templar strolled out towards it through the Casino gardens,
and above them the craggy head of old Pilatus loomed blackly
against a sky full of stars. At a jetty across the National-quai
a tourist launch was disgorging a load of trippers, and the
clear Swiss air was temporarily raucous with the alien accents
of Lancashire and London. Simon stood under a tree, enjoying a cigarette and waiting patiently for them to disperse. He
had a deep aversion to mobs, and did not want to walk in the
middle of one even the short distance to his hotel: something
perhaps overly sensitive and fastidious in him recoiled
instinctively from their mildly alcoholic exuberance and the
laughter that was just a shade too loud and shallow for his
tranquil mood. It was not because he was afraid of being
recognized. Any one of them would probably have reacted to
his name, or at least to his still better-known sobriquet, the
Saint; but none would have been likely to identify his face.
The features of the mocking buccaneer whose long and
simultaneous vendettas with the underworld and the law had
become legendary in his own life-time was known to few – a
fact which the Saint had often found to his advantage.

But at that moment he was not even thinking of the advan-
tages of anonymity. He was simply indulging a personal
distaste for boisterous holiday-makers. He was still trying to
take a holiday himself. He wanted nothing from them except
to be left alone, and they had nothing to fear from him.

Presently they were gone, and the esplanade was deserted again. He dropped his cigarette and stood like a statue, absorbed in the serene beauty of shimmering water and sentinel mountains.

From the direction of the Hotel National, off to his left, came a single set of footsteps. They were solid, purposeful, a little hurried. Simon turned only his head, and saw the man who made them as he came nearer – a stoutish man of middle height, wearing a dark suit and a dark homburg, carrying a bulky brief-case, the whole effect combined with his intent and urgent gait giving him an incongruously brisk and business-like appearance in the peaceful alpine night. Simon caught a glimpse of his face as he passed under one of the street lamps that stood along the water-front: it had a sallow and unmistakably Latin cast that was accentuated by a small pointed black beard.

Then, hardly a moment later, Simon realized that he was not watching one man, but three.

The other two came from somewhere out of the shadows – one tall and gaunt, the other short and powerful. They wore snap-brim hats pulled down over their eyes and kept their hands in their pockets. They, too, moved quickly and purposefully – more quickly even than the man with the beard, so that their distance behind him was dwindling rapidly. But the difference was that their feet made no sound . . .

It was so much like watching a conventional scene from a movie that for what seemed afterwards like an unforgivable length of time, but was probably no more than a number of seconds, the Saint observed it as passively as if he had been sitting in a theatre. Perhaps it was so obvious and implausible in that setting that his rational mind resisted accepting it at its face value. It was only as the two pursuers closed the last yard between them and the bearded man, and the lamplight flashed on steel in the gaunt one's hand, that Simon Templar understood that his immobility under the tree had let them think that they were unobserved, and that this was all for real. And by then there was no time left to forestall the climax of the act.

The two followers moved like a well co-ordinated team. The gaunt one's right hand snaked over their quarry's right shoulder and clamped over his mouth; the steel in his left hand disappeared where it touched the bearded man's back. At the same moment, like a horrible extension of the same creature, the stocky one snatched the brief-case out of unprotesting fingers. Then, in the same continuous flow of movement, the bearded man was falling bonelessly, like a rag doll, and the two attackers were running back towards the alley between the Casino gardens and the gardens of the Hotel National.

The tingle of belated comprehension was still crawling up the Saint's spine as he raced to intercept them. He did not call out, for it was too late now to warn the victim, and he saw no one else close enough to be any help. He ran as silently as the two footpads, and faster.

He met them at the corner of the alley. The gaunt one was nearer, and saw him first, and swung to meet him. The Saint saw a cruel bony face twisting in a vicious snarl, but he had the advantage of surprise. Before any of its transparently unfriendly intentions could materialize, his fist slammed into it, and the gaunt man sat down suddenly.

Either the stocky one was over-confident of his partner's ability to cope with the intrusion, or loyalty to a comrade was not in him, for he did not wait to lend his aid. He swerved and kept on running. And because he still carried the brief-case which appeared to be the prize in the affray, Simon ran after him.

The stocky one had an unexpected turn of speed for a man of his build. Reluctantly, because he was not dressed for it, the Saint launched himself in a flying tackle that just reached one of the stocky man's pistoning legs. The man fell lightly, like a wrestler, but Simon kept his grip on one ankle. Then, as they rolled over at the edge of a clump of rhododendrons, the man's other foot thumped into the side of the Saint's head. Coloured lights danced across Simon's eyes, and his hold loosened. He must have been half-stunned for a moment; then as his head cleared, he was holding nothing.

A heavy rustling in the bushes, hoarse shouts, and the sound of more running feet mingled confusedly in his brain as he sat up.

A man bent over him, only dimly visible in the gloom; and the Saint instinctively gathered himself to fight back before he realized that this was a new-comer. The height was about the same as that of the stocky man; but the silhouette, round and roly-poly, was different. The voice that came with it, in excellent English, with a curious mixture of Continental accent and Oxford vowels, was reassuring.

'Are you all right?'

Simon picked himself up, felt his face tenderly, and brushed off his clothes.

'I think so. Did you see my playmate?'

'He ran away. I'm not built for running – or football tackles. What was it about?'

There were more hurrying footsteps, and the beam of a flashlight stabbed at them. In the reflected glow behind it Simon saw the outlines of a uniform.

'Here's someone who's going to be professionally interested in the answer to that,' he said grimly.

The policeman spoke in the atrocious guttural dialect of the region. It was well out of the Saint's considerable linguistic range, but he needed no interpreter to translate it as some variant of the standard gambit of law officers in such situations anywhere: 'What goes on here?'

The roly-poly man answered in the same patois. His face in the light was round and soft and childish, with rimless glasses over rather prominent blue eyes. He wore a tweed coat and a round, soft pork-pie hat. He talked volubly, with graphic gestures, so that Simon easily understood that he was describing the Saint's encounter with the stocky thug, which he must have witnessed. The policeman asked another question, and the round man handed him a card from a small leather folder.

The policeman turned to the Saint.

'*Vous parlez français?*'

'*Mais oui,*' said the Saint easily. 'This gentleman saw me trying to catch one man. There was another. Over there.'

They walked to where Simon had dropped the gaunt man. But there was no one there.

'He seems to have got away, too,' he said ruefully. Then he pointed across the promenade. 'But there's the man they robbed.'

The gaunt man had taken back his knife, but it had done its work well. The man with the little black beard must have died almost instantly. His face was almost shockingly composed and disinterested when they turned him over.

'The brief-case which you say they took from him,' said the policeman, in French. 'What happened to it?'

Simon shrugged.

'I suppose the fellow I tackled got away with it.'

'And so we shall not know the motive for the attack,' observed the round man thoughtfully.

'Without wanting to play Sherlock Holmes,' said the Saint, with a trace of sarcasm, 'I should guess that it might have been robbery.'

The policeman was searching the pockets of the body. With a light touch on the arm, the moon-faced man drew the Saint a little aside.

'Restrain yourself, my friend. The police don't like to be teased. May I introduced myself? My name is Oscar Kleinhaus. I'm fairly well known here. I'll try to see that you have no trouble.'

'Thank you,' said the Saint curiously.

The policeman was holding an Italian passport.

'Filippo Ravenna,' he read from it. 'Of Venice. Married. Fifty-one years old. Director of companies.'

'Was he a friend of yours?' Kleinhaus asked.

'I never saw him before in my life,' said the Saint.

The policeman thumbed over the pages of the passport, and pointed at one of them.

'What is this?'

Simon looked over his shoulder.

'It's an immigrant's visa to the United States . . . issued a week ago. Apparently it has not yet been used.'

'But you say you did not know him.'

'I forget how many thousands of immigrants enter the United States every year,' said the Saint; 'but I assure you they are not all friends of mine.'

Again he felt a warning tug at his sleeve.

The rotund Mr Kleinhaus addressed the policeman again in his own dialect. He appeared to be arguing that the Saint was merely an innocent bystander who had tried to catch a couple of criminals; that he should not be treated like a suspect; that the policeman would do better to concentrate on the crime. The policeman seemed to be grudgingly impressed. He turned back to the Saint less aggressively.

'Your name, please?'

Simon had grown a little wary lately of the hazards of his reputation. In Switzerland, the traditional land of peace and neutrality, he had decided to make an attempt to reduce those risks when he registered at his hotel.

'Tombs,' he said. 'Sebastian Tombs.'

'Where are you staying here?'

'At the National.'

The policeman wrote down the information in a notebook.

For the first time, now, there were more people walking towards them along the quay. It was late, but presently there would be the inevitable crowd.

Kleinhaus said something else to the policeman, and the policeman seemed to agree. Kleinhaus took Simon by the arm and steered him away.

'We'll phone the station to send him some help,' he said. 'We can do it from your hotel. Could you identify those two thugs?'

'After a fashion.' Simon described them as best he could, as they walked through the gardens to the back entrance of the hotel. 'I suppose the detectives will want to know that, for what it's worth.'

'I'll pass it on to them when I telephone.' They were in the lobby. 'It'll be easier for me, speaking the lingo. And you don't want to get mixed up in it, and spoil your vacation. I'll take care of everything.'

Simon looked at him pensively.

'You're very kind,' he said. 'Is that just Swiss hospitality?'

'I don't like visitors to have had experiences in my country,' said Mr Kleinhaus. 'Go to bed. Perhaps we shall meet again.'

He raised his round hat courteously as Simon entered the elevator.

2

The Saint never stayed awake to ask himself questions to which he could only give himself imgainary answers. He slept as if nothing had happened, as if there were no loose ends in his mind, secure in the confidence that if the incident of that night was destined to be only a beginning it would reveal the rest of itself in its own good time. Life was like that for him. He did not have to seek adventure: his problem would have been to shake off its relentless pursuit.

He had just finished breakfast in his room when there was a knock on his door.

For anyone else, he reflected as he opened the door, it would probably have been only a waiter to take away the tray. For him, it had to be a woman. She was no more than thirty, beautiful in a dark classical way, like a Florentine painting, with a full figure that nullified the discretion of an expensive black dress. The deep shadows under her eyes were not out of a jar.

She said, with very little accent: 'Mr Tombs – may I talk to you? I am Mrs Ravenna.'

'Of course.'

She came in and sat down. Simon poured himself another cup of coffee and offered her a cigarette. She shook her head, and he lighted it for himself.

'I feel terribly guilty about your husband,' he said. 'I might have saved him. I just wasn't thinking fast enough.'

'At least you tried to catch the man who killed him. The police told me. I wanted to thank you.'

'I'm sorry I wasn't more successful. But if the police catch them, I may be able to identify them. I suppose you haven't any ideas about them?'

'I have none. Filippo was a good man. I didn't think he had any enemies.'

'Did he have business rivals?'

'I can't think of any. We were quite rich, but he was successful without hurting anyone. In any case, he had got rid of his interests.'

'What were they?'

'He manufactured shoes. It was a good business. But Europe today is an uncertain place. There is always fear – of war, of inflations, of unstable governments. So, we were going to America. Our quota number had just come through.'

'I know. And he was going to start a new business there?'

'Yes.'

'Well,' said the Saint, 'the police think it was just an ordinary robbery, don't they?'

'Yes.'

'Don't you?'

She twisted her fingers nervously together.

'I don't know what to think.'

The Saint stared at a plume of smoke drifting towards the ceiling. He tried half-heartedly not to recognize that his blood was suddenly running fast, in a way that had absolutely nothing to do with the young woman's appealing beauty. But it was no use. He knew, only too well, the symptoms of the almost psychic reflex that told him that he was in it again – up to the ears . . .

'I'm thinking,' he said slowly. 'These muggers didn't just pick your husband by accident. They knew what they were after. They didn't even try to look in his pockets. They just grabbed his brief-case and ran. Therefore they knew what was in it. What was that?'

'Some business papers, perhaps?'

'A shoe manufacturer would hardly be likely to have any trade secrets that would be worth going to those lengths to steal.'

'You talk like a detective.'

'Heaven forbid,' said the Saint piously. 'I'm only curious. What *did* he have in that brief-case?'

'I can't imagine.'

'It must have been something very valuable. And yet you know nothing about it?'

'No.'

She was lying, it was as obvious as the Alps; but he tried not to make it so obvious that he saw it.

'Why did you come here,' he asked, 'when you were just getting ready to move to America?'

'There were a few places we wanted to see before we left, because we didn't know if we would ever come back.'

'And yet, on a simple vacation trip like that, your husband brought along something so valuable that he could be murdered for it – and never even mentioned it to you?'

Her black eyes flashed suddenly hard like jet.

'You ask more questions than the police! Are you insulting me?'

'I'm sorry,' he said quickly. 'I was only trying to help. If we knew what was in that brief-case, we might have a clue to the people who stole it.'

She looked down at the twisting of her hands and made a visible effort to hold them still.

'Forgive me,' she said in a lowered voice. 'I am on edge. It has been such a shock . . . You are right. The brief-case is important. And that's really what I wanted to talk to you about. Those men – they did get it, didn't they?'

'Why, yes. I was chasing the man who had it. I brought him down, but he kicked me in the face and got away.'

'I thought perhaps he might have dropped it.'

'I didn't see it again.'

'Did the police search for it?'

'I don't think anyone would have. Even if the man dropped it he had plenty of time to pick it up again while I was knocked half silly. Anyway, it wasn't around. And if the police had found it, they'd certainly have returned it to you.'

Her eyes examined him uncertainly.

'If anyone found it . . . anyone . . . I would pay a large reward.'

'If I knew where to lay my hands on it,' said the Saint, a little frigidly, 'you wouldn't have to ask for it back, or pay any reward.'

She nodded.

'Of course. I'm being stupid. It was a foolish hope. Excuse me.' She stood up abruptly. 'Thank you for letting me talk to you – and again for what you tried to do. I must not bother you any more.'

She held out her hand and was gone.

Simon Templar stood where she had left him and slowly lighted another cigarette. Then he walked to the window. From the balcony outside he was offered a superb pano-rama of mountains rolling down to the sparkling blue foreground of the lake, where an excursion steamer swam like a toy trailing a brown veil of smoke; but irresistibly his eye was drawn downwards and to the right, towards the corner outside the gardens where he had tackled the stocky man.

He could have persuaded himself that it was only an illu-sion that he could see something from where he stood; but the echoes of the false notes that the Signora Ravenna had struck were less easy to dismiss.

He put on his jacket and went downstairs. After only a short search in the bushes near where he had tangled with the stocky men, he found the brief-case.

3

He figured it out as he took it upstairs to his room. The brief-case had indeed flown out of the stocky man's grasp when the Saint tackled him. It had fallen in among the rhododen-drons. Then Kleinhaus had come along, shouting. The stocky man had been too scared to stop and look for it. He had scrammed the hell out of there. The police hadn't looked for it, because they assumed it was gone. And the stocky man hadn't come back to look, either because he was afraid to or because he assumed the police would have found it.

And now the Saint had it.

He stood and looked at it for quite a while behind his locked door. He only had to pick up the telephone – he presumed that Signora Ravenna was staying in the same hotel – and tell her to come and get it. Or perhaps the more correct procedure would be to call the police. But either of these moves called for a man devoid of curiosity, a pillar of convention, a paragon of deafness to the siren voices of intrigue – which the Saint was not.

He opened it.

It required no instruments or violence. Just a steady pull on a zipper. It opened flat, exposing its contents in one dramatic revelation, as if they had been spread out on a tray.

Simon enumerated them as dispassionately as a catalogue, while another part of his mind fumbled woozily over trying to add them into an intelligible total.

Item: one chamois pouch containing a necklace of pink

pearls, perfectly graduated. Item: one hotel envelope containing eight diamonds and six emeralds, cut but unset, none less than two carats, each wrapped in a fold of tissue-paper. Item: a Cellophane envelope containing ten assorted postage stamps, of an age which suggested that they might be rare and valuable. Item: a book in an antique binding, which from the title pages appeared to be a first edition of Boccaccio's *Amorosa Visione*, published in Milan in 1521. Item: a small oil-painting on canvas without a frame, folded in the middle to fit the brief-case, but apparently protected from creasing by the bulk of the book, signed with the name of Botticelli. Item: a folded sheet of plain notepaper on which was typed in French:

M. Paul Galen
137 Wendenweg
Lucerne

Dear Monsieur Galen,
    The bearer, Signor Filippo Ravenna, can be trusted and his merchandise is most reliable.
                                    With best regards,

The signature was distinctive but indecipherable.

'And a fascinating line of merchandise it is,' brooded the Saint. 'For a shoemaker, Filippo must have been quite an interesting soul – or was he a heel? . . . A connoisseur and collector of very varied tastes? But, then, why should he bring his prize treasures with him on a trip like this? . . . A sort of Italian Raffles, leading a double life? But a successful businessman shouldn't need to steal. And if he did, his instincts would lead him to fancy book-keeping rather than burglary . . . A receiver of stolen goods? But then he wouldn't need a formal introduction to someone else who sounds as if he might be in that line of business ... And what a strange assortment of loot! There has to be a clue there, if I could find it ...'

But for ten minutes the significance eluded him. And at that point he gave up impatiently.

There was another clue, more positive, more direct in the letter to the mysterious Paul Galen; and it was one which should not be too difficult to run down.

He put the jewels, the stamps, and the letter in different pockets of his coat. The book and the painting, too bulky to carry inconspicuously, he put back in the brief-case and zippered it up again. He hid it, not too seriously, under the mattress at the head of the bed. Then, with a new lightness in his step, he went out and rang for the elevator.

It took him down one floor, and stopped again. Signora Ravenna got in.

For the space of one skipped heartbeat he wondered whether her room, too, might have a balcony from which she might have watched him retrieve the brief-case from the bushes below; but he met her eyes with iron coolness and only a slight pleasant nod to acknowledge their acquaintance, and his pulse resumed smoothly when she gave back only a small perfunctory smile.

She had put on a small black hat and carried a purse.

'The police have asked me to go and talk to them again,' she volunteered. 'They have thought of more questions, I suppose. Did they send for you, too?'

'I haven't heard from them since last night,' he said. 'But I expect they'll get around to me eventually.'

It occurred to him that it was a little odd that he had not been asked to repeat the descriptions which Oscar Kleinhaus had promised to relay; but he was too busy with other thoughts to speculate much about the reasons for it. He was grateful enough to have been dropped out of the investigation.

As they strolled across the lobby he said: 'Will you think me impertinent if I ask another question?'

'No,' she said. 'I want your help.'

'When your husband went out last night – did he say where he was going?'

She answered mechanically, so that he knew she was reciting something that she had said before.

'I was tired, and he wanted to look for a café where he had heard there were Tyrolean singers, so he went alone.'

'Didn't you think it strange that he should take his brief-case?'

'I didn't see him take it.'

Simon handed her into a taxi without another word.

He walked slowly towards the Schweizerhof. At the corner of the Alpenstrasse he bought a selection of morning papers, and sat down at the nearest café over a cup of chocolate to read methodically through all the headlines.

He had just finished when a shadow fell across the table, and a familiar voice said: 'Looking to see whether you are a hero, Mr Tombs?'

It was Oscar Kleinhaus, and the disarming smile on his cherubic face made his remark innocent of offence. The Saint smiled back, no less disarmingly.

'I was rather curious to see what the newspapers said about it,' he admitted. 'But they don't seem to have the story yet.'

'No, I didn't notice it either. I'm afraid our Press is a little slow by American standards. We think that if a story would be good in the morning it will be just as interesting in the evening.'

'Would you care to join me?'

Kleinhaus shook his head.

'Unfortunately I have a business appointment. I hope I'll have another opportunity. How long are you staying here?'

'I haven't made any plans. I thought the police would want to know that, but no one's been near me.'

'If they caught anyone for you to identify, they would want you. Until then I expect they think it more considerate not to trouble you. But if you asked for your bill at the hotel, I'm sure they would be informed.' The round face was completely bland and friendly. 'I must go now. But we shall run into each other again. Lucerne is a small town.'

He raised his collegiate hat with the same formal courtesy as the night before, and ambled away.

Simon watched him very thoughtfully until he was out of sight. Then he hailed a cab and gave the address which he had found in the brief-case.

The road turned off the Alpenstrasse above the ancient ramparts of the old town and wound up the hillside with ever-widening vistas of the lake into a residential district of neat doll-house chalets. The house where the taxi stopped was high up, perched out on a jutting crag; and Simon had paid off the driver and was confirming the number on the door, with his finger poised over the bell, before he really acknowledged to himself that he had already had two wide-open and obvious opportunities to speak about the brief-case to more or less interested parties since he had found it, and that he had studiously ignored both of them – not to mention that he had made no move whatever to report his discovery to the police. But now he could no longer pretend to be unaware of what he was doing. And it is this chronicler's shocking duty to record that the full and final realization gave him a lift of impenitent exhilaration which the crisp mountain air could never have achieved alone.

The door opened and a manservant with a seamed grey face, dressed in sombre black, looked him over impersonally.

'Is Monsieur Galen here?' Simon inquired.

'*De la part de qui, m'sieur?*'

'I am Filippo Ravenna,' said the Saint.

4

The room into which he was ushered was large and sunny, furnished with the kind of antiques that look priceless and yet comfortable to live with. The walls on either side of the fireplace were lined with bookshelves, on two others were paintings and a tapestry, in the fourth french windows opened on to a terrace overlooking the town and the mountains and the lake. The carpet underfoot was Aubusson. It was the living-room of a man of wealth and cheerful good taste, and the manservant looked like an undertaker in it, but he withdrew as soon as he had shown the Saint in.

The man who advanced to greet Simon was altogether different. He had a muscular build rounded with good living, a full crop of black hair becomingly flecked with silver, and strong, fleshy features. White teeth gleamed around a cigar.

'Buon giorno, Signor! Sono felicissimo di vederla.'

'We can speak French if you prefer,' said the Saint cautiously. It was safer than trying to speak Italian as a native tongue.

'As you wish. Or German, or English even. I struggle with all of them. I want my clients to feel comfortable, and they come from so many places.' He waved Simon to a couch facing the windows. 'You have a letter, perhaps?'

Simon handed him the introduction. Galen glanced at it and put it in his pocket and sat down.

'I knew you were coming,' he said apologetically, 'but it is necessary to be careful.'

'Of course.'

'Sometimes my clients are so preoccupied with evading their own export restrictions that they forget we have Swiss import regulations, too. That is their own affair, but naturally I want no trouble with the authorities here.'

'I understand your position,' said the Saint, understanding very little.

'Worse still,' Galen said talkatively, 'there are people who try to offer me stolen things. That is why it is so pleasant to meet someone who is recommended like yourself. Aside from the risk involved with stolen property, it is so much trouble to sell, and the prices are bound to be miserable. It is not worth it.'

Simon nodded sympathetically, while his brain seemed to flounder in an intangible quicksand. So the eccentric assortment of treasures in Ravenna's brief-case were supposed to be his own legitimate property, which finally disposed of one theory, but at the same time cut away one possible piece of solid ground. Why, then, all the secrecy and mystery?

The Saint said conversationally: 'So your clients come from all over Europe, do they?'

'From everywhere between the Iron Curtain and Portugal – every country where there are these annoying restrictions on foreign exchange and the free movement of wealth. What a pity there have to be so many barriers in this primitive civilization! However, I have a nice central location, and Swiss money is good anywhere in the world. Also, I am very discreet. There is no law here against me buying anything I choose, and not a word about our transaction will get back to Italy from me. Other people's problems are my business opportunity, but I prefer to think of myself as a kind of liberator.' He laughed genially. 'Now, what do you have to sell?'

Simon gave him the chamois bag.

Galen took out the pink pearl necklace and held it up to
the light.

'It is beautiful,' he said admiringly.

He studied it more closely, and then pondered for several
seconds while he carefully evened the ash on his cigar.

'I can give you four hundred thousand Swiss francs,' he
said at length. 'Or, if you like, the equivalent in dollars, deposited at any bank in New York. That would be something over
seventeen thousand dollars. It is a good price in the circumstances.' He draped the necklace over his fingers and admired
it again; then his shrewd dark eyes turned back to the Saint.
'But it is not a lot of capital for you to start building a new
fortune in America. Surely you have some other things to
offer me?'

Simon Templar took an infinitesimal moment to reply.
And in that apocalyptic instant he realized that he had found
a foothold again with a suddenness that literally jarred the
breath out of him.

It was all so simple, so obvious, that in retrospect he
wondered how it could ever have baffled him. Filippo Ravenna
had been going to America to live and to make a fresh start.
Ravenna was rich, but he would not be allowed to transfer all
his assets across the Atlantic just by asking for a bank draft.
Like many another European, he had nothing but money,
which was not translatable through ordinary channels. But
someone had told him about Paul Galen. So Ravenna had
bought things. Things whose only connecting characteristics
were that they were relatively small, relatively light in weight,
relatively easy to smuggle, and very valuable; things, moreover,
which a man in his position could acquire without attracting
undue attention. And he had brought them to Switzerland to
convert back into hard money – with an introduction to Paul
Galen, who had made an international business out of co-operating in such evasions, whose reputation in such tricky-minded

circles was doubtless a guarantee of comparatively fair dealing and absolute discretion.

All that part of it was dazzlingly clear; and the other part was starting to grow clearer – some of it, at least.

The Saint found himself saying, almost absentmindedly: 'I left the other things at the hotel. You understand, I thought we should get acquainted first.'

Somewhere outside the room he was aware of indistinct voices, but it was a rather sub-conscious impression which he only recalled afterwards, for at the moment it did not seem that they could concern him.

'I hope I have made a good impression,' Galen said with lively good humour. 'What else did you bring?'

'I have a small Botticelli,' said the Saint slowly. He was stalling for time really, while his mind raced ahead from the knowledge it now had to fit together the pieces that still had to tie in. 'It is a museum piece. And a first edition of Boccaccio, in perfect condition—'

The door behind him burst open as if a tornado had struck it, and that was when he actually remembered the premonitory sounds of argument that he had heard.

It was the Signora Ravenna, with her bosom heaving and her black eyes blazing with dark fire. Behind her followed the funeral manservant, looking apologetically helpless.

'Go on,' she said. 'What else was there?'

Galen was on his feet as quickly as a big dog. He glanced at the Saint with quizzical wariness as Simon stood up more leisurely.

'Do you know this lady?'

'Certainly,' said the Saint calmly. 'She is Signora Ravenna.'

Galen almost relaxed.

'A thousand pardons. You should have told me your wife—'

'I am not his wife,' the young woman cut him short passionately. 'My husband was murdered last night, by robbers who stole his brief-case with the things he brought to sell. This impostor is an American who calls himself Tombs – he is probably the employer of the men who killed my husband!'

Galen moved easily around the couch, without apparent haste or agitation.

'That is quite an extraordinary statement,' he remarked temperately. 'But no doubt one of you can at least prove your identity.'

'I can,' said Signora Ravenna. She fumbled in her hand-bag. 'I can show you my passport. Ask him to show you his!'

'I'll save you the trouble,' said the Saint, amiably in English. 'I concede that this is Signora Ravenna, and it's true that she's been a widow for about twelve hours.'

'Then your explanation had better be worth listening to,' Galen said in the same language.

It was produced so smoothly and casually that Simon never knew where it came from, but now there was an auto-matic in Galen's hand, the muzzle lined up with Simon's midriff. The melancholy manservant remained in the door-way, and somehow he no longer looked apologetic.

Simon's gaze slid languidly over the barrel of the gun and up to Galen's coldly questioning face. It was no performance that he scarcely seemed to notice the weapon. He was too happy with the way the other fragments of the puzzle were falling into place to care.

'I happened to see Signor Ravenna jumped on last night by two thugs who stole his brief-case,' he said. 'I imagine he was on his way to see you then. I tried to catch them, but I didn't do so good. There's an independent witness, a local citizen, who saw me try, and he's on record with the police ... This morning Signora Ravenna came to my room and asked me about the brief-case. She said she had no idea what was in it and couldn't imagine why anyone would attack her husband. I told her that so far as I knew the thieves had got away with it.'

'A bluff, to try to make it look as if they weren't working for you,' Signora Ravenna said vehemently. 'You had it all the time!'

'I didn't,' said the Saint easily. 'But, after you left, I went on thinking. It occurred to me that there was just an outside chance that the fellow I nearly caught had dropped it, and then nobody had thought of looking for it – everybody taking it for granted that somebody else had got it. I went back to the spot and looked. Sure enough, there it was in the bushes. I took it back to my room.'

'You see, he admits it! I saw him again after that, and he didn't say anything about finding it. He meant to steal it all the time. The only thing he doesn't confess is that the whole thing was planned!'

'While Signora Ravenna was asking me questions,' Simon continued imperturbably, 'I also asked her a few. And I knew damned well she was lying. That made me curious. So I opened the brief-case. I found the painting, the book, the necklace which you have – and of course, that letter of introduction to you. It was just too much for my inquisitive nature. So I came here, using Ravenna's name, to try and find out what was going on. You've been kind enough to explain the background to me. I now know that Ravenna was simply trying to turn his assets into American money which he could use when he emigrated – which, you've explained to me, isn't a crime here, whatever they think of it in Italy. So I'm satisfied about that – but not about why Signora Ravenna told me so many lies.'

'I leave that to you, Monsieur Galen,' said the woman with a triumphant shrug. 'I would not even tell the police, still less a perfect stranger.'

Galen's dispassionate eyes rested immovably, on the Saint's face.

'And what is your business, Mr Tombs?'

'Just think of me,' said the Saint, 'as a guy with a weakness for puzzles, and an incorrigible asker of questions. I have a few more.' He looked at Signora Ravenna again. 'Are you positive your husband couldn't have discussed this deal with anyone?'

'Only with his best friend, who gave him the introduction to Monsieur Galen.'

'And you're sure you never mentioned it to anybody?'

'Of course not.'

'But as I said this morning, the jokers who waylaid your husband knew he was carrying something valuable, and even knew it was in his brief-case. How do you account for that?'

'I don't know how crooks like you find out these things,' she flared. 'Why don't you tell us?'

Simon shook his head.

'I suggest,' he said rather forensically, 'that those crooks could only have known because you told them – because you hired them to get rid of your husband and bring you back his most negotiable property.'

The servant in the doorway was pushed suddenly aside, and a short spherical man elbowed his way unceremoniously past him into the room.

'I am Inspector Kleinhaus, of the police,' he said, 'and I should also like to hear the answer to that.'

5

'You see,' he explained diffidently, 'we had a friendly tip from Italy that two known Italian criminals had bought tickets to Switzerland. It was my job to keep an eye on them. I'm afraid they gave me the slip last night, for long enough to attack and rob Signor Ravenna. When I met you at the scene of the crime, Mr Tombs, I didn't know if you might be associated with them, so I didn't introduce myself completely. But we kept watch on you. We saw you find the brief-case and take it to your room – incidentally, we recovered it as soon as you went out, with its interesting contents.'

Galen put the automatic in his pocket and took out the necklace.

'Except this,' he said conscientiously.

'Thank you,' said Kleinhaus. 'Meanwhile, Mr Tombs, we went on keeping an eye on you, to see where you'd lead us. I still didn't know how deeply you were involved in the affair, and I was puzzled as you seem to have been by the things Ravenna was carrying and by the motive for the robbery. Most of that has now been cleared up. One of my men followed you here, and I followed Signora Ravenna myself after I talked to her at the police station a little while ago. Her answers seemed as suspicious to me as they apparently did to you.'

'How long have you been listening?' Simon asked.

'Monsieur Galen's servant was too agitated by the way

Signora Ravenna behaved when he told her her husband was already here to remember to shut the front door, so I've been in the hall all the time. It was very illuminating.' The detective's blue eyes shifted again. 'Now, Signora Ravenna, I still want to hear what you were going to say.'

Her face was a white mask.

'I have nothing to say! You can't be serious about such an accusation – and from such a person! Can you believe I would have my own husband murdered?'

'Such things have happened,' Kleinhaus said sadly. 'However, we can check in another way. I'm glad to be able to tell you now that the two men have already been caught. Mr Tombs will be able to identify them. Then you can confront them, and we'll see what they say when they realize there's only one way to save their own skins.'

It was pitiful to see the false indignation drain out of her face, and the features turn ugly and formless with terror. She moistened her lips, and her throat moved, but no sound came. And then, as if she understood that in that silence she had already betrayed her own guilt for all to see, she gave an inarticulate little cry and ran past Galen, shoving him out of the way with a hysterical violence that sent him staggering, and ran out through the french windows, out on to the sunlit terrace that went to the edge of the cliff where the house perched, and kept on running . . .

Inspector Kleinhaus, presently, was the first to turn from looking down over the edge. With a conclusive gesture he replaced his absurdly juvenile hat.

'Perhaps that saves a lot of unpleasantness,' he remarked. 'Well, I must still ask you to identify the two men, Mr Tombs – your name really is Tombs, is it?'

'It sounds sort of ominous, doesn't it?' said the Saint easily.

He still had eight diamonds, six emeralds, and ten valuable stamps in his pockets which no one was left to ask embarrassing questions about, and at such a time it would have been very foolish to draw any more attention to himself.

Juan-Les-Pins
The Spanish Cow

INTRODUCTION BY LESLIE CHARTERIS*

There are just a few stories which I genuinely regret losing, which were lost by force of circumstance and which I can do nothing about. They were all original Saint stories too, and I was thinking of them while working on a new collection of shorter pieces which I am now trying to finish up.

... also there was a story about the Saint's vengeance on an absconding company promoter, readable but not particularly distinguished; and a story called The Spanish Cow, the only recorded instance where the Saint deliberately played gigolo with a covetous eye on a fat old woman's jewels, but with a most unpredictable denouement. The manuscripts of these I have lost somewhere: nobody else could find them except me, and I don't seem to be able to. Nor do I have the heart to try and write them again from memory. There is nothing so dead to me as a story that has been written once and left behind. These are like children that died young: it's too bad we can't have them with us today, but there would be something zombie-like about their resurrection, and so we can only write them off and devote ourselves to the more positively entertaining business of making new ones.

(Editorial note: Needless to say, this was also revived ...)

* From *A Letter from the Saint* (1947)

I

'People,' said Myra Campion languidly, 'ought to have to pass an examination and get licensed before they're allowed to exhibit themselves on a bathing beach.'

Simon Templar smiled vaguely and trickled sand through his fingers. Around them spread the sun-baked shambles of Juan-les-Pins – a remarkable display of anatomy in the raw. As far as the eye could see in either direction, men and women of all nationalities, ages, shapes, sizes, and shades of colour, stripped to the purely technical minimum of covering demanded by the liberal laws of France, littered themselves along the landscape and wooed the ultra-violet ray with a unanimous concentration of effort that would have restored world prosperity if it had been turned into the channels of banking or breeding pedigree wombats or some such lucrative field of endeavour. Reclining on straw mats, under beach umbrellas, in deck chairs, or even on the well-worn sand itself, they sprawled along the margin of that fashionable stretch of water in a sizzling abandon of scorched flesh that would have made a hungry cannibal lick his lips. To the Saint's occasionally cynical eye there was something reminiscent of an orgy of human sacrifice in that welter of burnt-offerings on the altar of the snobbery of tan. Sometimes he thought that a keen ear might have heard the old sun-god's homeric laughter at the childish sublimation that had repopulated his shrine, as the novices turned themselves like joints on a spit, basted their blistered skin with oils and creams, and lay down to roast again, suffering patiently that they might triumph in the end. Simon looked at teak-bronzed males with beautifully lubricated hair parading themselves in magnificent disdain amongst the pink and peeling and furtively envious new-comers; and, being as brown as they were, only larger minded, he was amused.

But not at the moment. At the moment he was interested exclusively in Mrs Porphyria Nussberg.

Mrs Nussberg, at that moment, was methodically divesting herself of a set of boned pink corsets, preparatory to having her swim. The corsets were successfully removed under cover of her dress, defiantly rolled up, and deposited in her canvas chair. The dress followed; and Mrs Nussberg was revealed in a bright yellow bathing costume of nineteenth-century cut, which rose to the base of her neck and extended itself along her limbs almost to the knees and elbows. The completion of her undressing was hailed with irreverent applause from several parties in her neighbourhood.

'I wonder,' said Myra Campion languidly, making her observation more particular in all the arrogance of her own golden slenderness, 'how that woman has the nerve to come here.'

'Maybe it amuses her,' suggested the Saint lazily, with his blue eyes narrowed against the sun. 'Why do fat men feel an urge to wear check suits?'

His vagueness was rather an illusion. As a matter of fact he was quite pleasantly conscious of the slim blonde grace of the girl beside him; but he had the gift of splitting his mind between two distinct occupations, and one half of his mind had been revolving steadily around Mrs Nussberg and Mrs Nussberg's jewels for several days.

Of the late Mr Nussberg he knew little, except that he had lived in Detroit and manufactuered metal buttons for attach-ment to cheap overalls, and had in due course died, full of

honour and indigestible food. Simon rather suspected that he
had been a small man with a bald head and baggy trousers, but
he admitted that this suspicion was based on nothing more
substantial than the theory that women of Mrs Nussberg's size
and demeanour are usually married by small men with bald
heads and baggy trousers. The point was purely academic,
anyway: it was now Porphyria Nussberg who carried the
burden of a reputedly fabulous fortune on her massive shoulders, and whose well-padded physique, which in some respects
did actually resemble that of a camel, should have been specu-
lating anxiously about the size of the needle's eye through
which it might one day be called upon to pass.

Mrs Nussberg had arrived on the same day as the Saint
himself; but she had since become far better known. She was
popularly referred to by a variety of names, of which 'The
Queen of Sheba', 'Cleopatra', and 'The American Tragedy'
were a fairly representative selection. But to Simon Templar
she would always be the Spanish Cow.

From this it should not be hastily assumed that the Saint
was unnecessarily vulgar. To those of cosmopolitan education, the Spanish Cow is an allusion hardly less classical than
others that had been bestowed upon Porphyria. The Spanish
Cow – *la vache espagnol* – is, curiously enough, a creature of
the French mythology, and is indignantly repudiated by
Spain. It is the symbol of everything clumsy, inefficient, and
absurd. When a Frenchman wishes to say that he speaks
English excessively badly, he will tell you that he speaks
comme une vache espagnol – like a Spanish Cow. In the same
simile he may dance, play bridge, butt into a petting party, or
remember that he owes you a few thousand francs. For the
benefit of those in search of higher education, it might be
explained that this does not stem from any ancient national
antagonism or occult anthropomorphic legend; it is, etymo-
logically, a corruption of *Basque espagnol*, and originated in

the belief of French purists that the Basques speak atro-
ciously; but this is not the place to enter that argument. To
Simon, the name fitted Mrs Nussberg like a glove with a
pleasing ambivalence that included her swarthy complexion
and distinctly bovine build.

She waddled on towards the water's edge through a cloud
of giggles, grins, and whispered comments that were pitched
just loud enough to reach her ears; and Simon kicked his toes
through the sand and gazed after her thoughtfully. The daily
baiting of the Spanish Cow had lost most of its novelty as a
spectacle, for him; though the rest of the beach showed no
signs of tiring of it. It had already rivalled water ski-ing among
the sports of that season. It had the priceless advantage of
costing nothing, and of giving a satisfactory reaction to the
most awkward tyro. Goaded far enough, Mrs Nussberg could
always be relied upon to give a demonstration in return which
dissolved the onlookers into shrieks of laughter. It happened,
according to plan, that morning. As Mrs Nussberg tested the
temperature of the water with her toes, the Adonis of the beach
came swaggering along the rim of the wet sand, rippling his
rounded muscles – Maurice Walmar, heir to millions and one
of the oldest titles in the *Almanac de Gotha*, a privileged person
at any time, and the most daring leader of the new sport. His
dark sensual eyes took in the situation at once, and a smile
touched his lips. He fell on his knees and bowed his head to the
ground in an elaborate mockery of homage.

Mrs Nussberg put out her tongue at him. The beach
howled with delight.

'She must be screwy,' opined Myra Campion, fascinated.

The opinion was pretty generally held. Properly provoked,
Mrs Nussberg could be depended on to pull the most horrible faces at her tormentors, squawk abuse at them like a
trained parrot, and even put her fingers to her nose. Far from
bringing forbearance, that apparent screwiness seemed to

fan a spark of pure sadism in the onlookers – the same savage instinct that impels urchins to throw stones at an idiot village boy.

'Have you seen that caricature of her outside the Fregate?' asked Miss Campion. 'The boy who draws portraits on the beach did it. It's too perfect. She tried to make them take it down, and they said she could have it if she bought it. They told her she could have it for fifty thousand francs, but it's still there. In a frame, hanging up in the entrance.'

'I'll have to take a look at it,' said the Saint. He stood up, dusting the sand from his legs. 'Do you think you could get around that buoy again before lunch?'

As he slid easily through the cool smooth water he looked back and saw the bright yellow bathing cap of the Spanish Cow bobbing in the sunlight close to the shore, as she paddled about with her clumsy breast stroke. He pillowed his face in the blue sea and drifted on with a sweep of long effortless arms, down through the crystalline transparency to the misty depths, gazing where tiny fish flicked and turned like silver sparks, and decided that the time was ripe for Mrs Nussberg and her jewels to meet Romance.

2

It all began the day after Simon arrived at Juan-les-Pins. He was sitting on a high stool in a sandwich bar, refreshing his interior with a glass of iced orange juice, when the Spanish Cow came in. Simon did not then know her real name, nor had he become sufficiently interested to christen her but, observing that she wore voluminous beach pyjamas with broad horizontal stripes of purple and yellow, which made her look like a great blowsy wasp, it is probable that some of the emotion he felt might have been detected by an eagle eye. The Saint's sense of humour was very human; and the barman looked at him and grinned sympathetically, as one who in his day had also been confronted by the spectacle for the first time. It is therefore possible that the Saint's face was not quite so woodenly disciplined as a meticulous politeness might have wished. It is possible that one of his eyebrows twitched involuntarily, or the corners of his mouth widened a slight half-millimetre, in answer to the barman's confidence. And then he glanced at the vision again, and saw that it was staring at him through a pair of lorgnettes and pulling faces at him.

The Saint blinked. He regarded his orange juice suspiciously. To a man of his abstemious habits, it was a remarkable hallucination to affront the brain at eleven o'clock in the morning – even in a morning of such potent sunshine as those shores boast in July.

He looked again. Mrs Nussberg put out her tongue in a grimace of bloodcurdling menace.

Simon swayed slightly on his stool. His friends had frequently told him that he was quite mad, but he had never expected to lose his last vestige of sanity in quite so disturbing a way. He turned uneasily to an inspection of the other patrons of the bar, wondering if the portly Dutchman on his left would suddenly seem to be elongating and turning bight green, or if the charming honey-blonde damsel on his right would be pulling off her pink ears and stirring them into her coffee. Instead he found the other customers still of normal shape and hue, smiling broadly. He braced himself to look at the striped vision again. It applied its thumb to its nose and extended its fingers towards him, waggling them with hideous glee.

The charming damsel on his right spoke, through the daze of alarm that was rapidly enveloping him.

'Don't pay any attention to her,' she said. 'She's always like that.'

'Bless you, darling,' murmured the Saint fervently. 'For a moment I thought the heat had got me.'

'Who's always like what?' screamed Mrs Nussberg.

The charming damsel sipped her coffee.

'We're off,' she remarked.

'I can pull faces just as well as you can,' yelled Mrs Nussberg with justifiable pride; and the little imps of Satan elected that instant to enter into the Saint.

He turned.

'Madam,' he said generously, 'you can pull them better.'

Simon had never spoken boastfully of the encounter. He was ordinarily a very chivalrous bloke, kind to the fat and infirm and willing to oblige a lady in any manner that was in his power; but there were moments when he ceased to be a truly responsible captain of his soul and that was one of them.

The result was that three minutes later he found himself strolling back to the beach with the charming damsel on his arm and a delirious bar behind him. Few people had ever been known to score off the Saint in an exchange of back-chat, and Mrs Nussberg was certainly not one of them. It was that same night, in the Casino, that he saw Mrs Nussberg plastered with all her jewels, and the modest glow of those three minutes of light-headed revelry abruptly vanished.

Which explained his abstracted thoughtfulness on this subsequent morning.

For it was a principle of the Saint's sparsely principled career that one never exchanged entirely carefree badinage with anyone so liberally adorned with diamonds as Mrs Porphyria Nussberg. On the contrary, one tended to be patient – almost long-suffering. Following the example of the sun-worshippers simmering in their grease, one stewed to conquer. Diamonds so large and plentiful could not be gazed upon at any time by any honest filibuster without sentiment; and when they chanced to be hung around a woman who pulled faces and shouted wrathfully across bars, it became almost a sacred duty to give that sentiment full rein. Unfortunately, Simon saw the grimaces first and the jewel-lery afterwards; and he had spent some days regretting that chance order of events – the more earnestly when he discov-ered that Myra Campion had helped to spread the fame of his achievement, and that he was widely expected to repeat the performance every time he and Mrs Nussberg passed close enough to speak.

He hoped speechlessly that the call of Romance, which he had at last decided was the only possible approach, might be strong enough to obliterate the memory of that earlier argu-ment. The Spanish Cow had no friends – he had had some difficulty in learning her official name which no one had apparently troubled to inquire. From local gossip he learned that she had once had a gigolo, a noisome biped with tinted fingernails and a lisp; but even that specimen had found the penalties of his job too high, and had minced on to pastures less conspicuous. It seemed as if a cavalier with stamina to last the course might get near enough to those lavish ropes of gems to pay his expenses; and having reached that decision Simon made up his mind to go ahead with it before his nerve failed him.

He had his chance at the Casino that evening. Miss Campion was safely settled at the *boule* table with a pile of chips, and the Saint looked around and saw Mrs Nussberg emerging majestically from the baccarat-room and proceeding towards a table in the lounge. Simon drew a deep breath, straightened his tie, and sauntered after her.

She stared at him belligerently.

'What do you want?'

'I think I owe you an apology,' said the Saint quietly.

'You've found that out, have you?' she barked.

A smirking waiter was dusting off the table. Simon sat down opposite her and ordered a *fine à-l'eau*. Parties at adjoining tables were already glancing curiously and expectantly towards them, and the movement cost Simon a clammier effort than anything he had done for a long time.

'That morning – a few days ago,' he explained contritely. 'You misunderstood me. I wasn't being fresh. But when you called me down I sort of forgot myself.'

'I should think you did,' rasped Mrs Nussberg without friendliness.

'I'm sorry.'

'So you ought to be.'

It dawned on the Saint that this vein of dialogue could be continued almost indefinitely if Mrs Nussberg insisted on it. He looked around somewhat tensely for inspiration, wondering if, after all, the jewels could be worth the price; and by the mercy of his guardian angel the inspiration was provided.

It was provided in the person of Maurice Walmar, who at

that moment came strolling superbly across the lounge and recognized an acquaintance in the far corner. With an elegant wave of his hand he started in that direction. His route took him past the table where Simon was prayerfully groping for the light. Walmar recognized the Spanish Cow, and flashed a meaning sneer towards his acquaintance. As he squeezed past the table, he deliberately swerved against Mrs Nussberg's arm as she raised her glass. The drink spilled heavily across her lap.

'*Pardon*,' said Walmar casually, and went on.

Simon leapt up.

Even if he had not been interested in Mrs Nussberg's jewels, he would probably have done the same thing. He had witnessed every phase of the incident, and at any time he would have called that carrying a joke too far. Nor did he care much for Maurice Walmar, with his too-beautifully modelled face and platinum watch bracelet. He caught the young humorist by the elbow and spun him around.

'I don't think you saw what you did,' he remarked evenly.

For a second the other was startled to incredulity. Then he glanced down at the soaked ruin of Mrs Nussberg's gown, and back from that to the Saint. His aristocratic lips curled in their most polished insolence.

'I have apologized,' he said carelessly. 'It was an accident.'

'Then so is this,' said the Saint mildly, and his fist shot over and slammed crisply into the centre of the sneering mouth.

Walmar rocked on his heels. He clutched at a table and went down in a spatter of glass and splashing fluids.

There was an instant's deathly stillness; and then a grey-haired Englishman observed quietly: 'He asked for it.'

Walmar crawled up shakily. His mouth was a mess and there was blood on his silk shirt. A covey of waiters awoke from their momentary stupor and buzzed in among the tables, interposing themselves between a resumption of the strife. The players abandoned the *boule* table and swarmed out towards the prospect of more primitive sport, leaving the high priest to intone his forlorn '*Rien ne va plus!*' to a skeleton congregation. The two inevitable policemen, who appear as if at the rubbing of a kind of Aladdin's lamp on the scene of any French fracas, stalked ponderously into the perspective, closely followed by an agitated manager. The tableau had all the makings of a second-act musical-comedy curtain, but Simon overcame the temptation to explore all the avenues of extravagant burlesque which it opened up. He spoke calmly and to the point.

'He upset this lady's drink – purposely.'

Walmar, struggling dramatically in the grasp of a waiter whom he could have shaken off with a wave of his hand, shouted: 'Messieurs! It was an accident. He attacked me—'

The larger *agent* turned to the waiter.

'*Qu'est-ce qui est arrivé?*' he demanded.

'*Je n'ai rien vu,*' answered the man tactfully.

It was the grey-haired Englishman who came forward with quiet corroboration, and the affair turned into a general soothing party for Maurice Walmar whose wealth and family entitled him to eccentricities that would rapidly have landed an ordinary visitor in jail. The jaundiced eye with which private battles are viewed in France was well known to the Saint, and he was rather relieved to be spared the unheroic sequels in which offenders against the code of peace are usually involved.

He went out on to the terrace with Mrs Nussberg, and as he left the lounge he caught sight of Myra Campion's face among the spectators who were staring after him in the pained blank manner of a row of dowagers who have been simultaneously bitten in the fleshy part of the leg by their favourite Pomeranians. Miss Campion's sweet symmetrical features were almost egg-like in their stupefied bewilderment; and Simon's smile as he reached the edge of the balcony and looked out over the dark sea came quite naturally.

'You've seen for yourself,' he said. 'I've just got a natural gift for getting into trouble.'

'Served him right,' blared Mrs Nussberg. 'The dirty little—'

Her comment on Maurice Walmar's lineage was certainly inaccurate, but Simon could understand her feelings.

The orchestra wailed into another erotic symphony, and the Saint expanded his chest and flicked his cigarette over the parapet. The job had to be completed.

'Would you like to dance?' he asked.

The Spanish Cow gazed at him suspiciously, her small eyes hard and bright in the sallow, puffy face. Then, without answering, she marched towards the floor.

As they completed their first circle under the fairy lights Simon saw that the colony was following his movements with bulging eyes. It went into small huddles and buzzed, as openly as convention would permit. He began to find more innocent entertainment in his sudden notoriety than he had ever expected – and the Saint had never found the appalled reactions of respectable society dull. There were times when he derived a purely urchin satisfaction from the flouting of the self-appointed Best People, and he was quite disappointed when the Spanish Cow broke away from him after a half-dozen turns.

'I can't stay here with my dress soaking,' she said abruptly. 'Take me home.'

Simon walked back with her to the Provençal. The sky was a blaze of star-dust, and a whisper of music came from the Casino terrace. Down by the water there were tiny ripples hissing and chattering on the firm sand, and a light breeze murmured in the fronds of the tall palms. Simon had a fleeting remembrance of the slim, exquisite softness of Myra

Campion; and, being very human, he sighed inaudibly. But business was business.

A few yards from the hotel entrance Mrs Nussberg stopped. Her ropes of diamonds flashed in the light of the rows of bulbs flaming the marquee over the doors.

'Thank you for helping me,' she said with a harsh effort.

Simon's teeth flashed. He knew that she was taking stock of his tanned, keen-lined face, the set of his wide shoulders and the length of lean muscular limbs. He knew that he was interesting to look at – conquering a natural bashfulness that he always kept well under control, he admitted the fact frankly.

'Not at all,' he said.

She opened her bag and held something out to him. He took it and unfolded it – it was a ten-thousand-franc note. He folded it again carefully and handed it back with a smile.

'I'm afraid you're mistaken,' he said pleasantly. 'You don't owe me anything. Good night.'

3

There began for Mrs Porphyria Nussberg an interlude of peace that must have been strange to her. The glances that she encountered veiled their derision with perplexed uncertainty; the giggles when she unharnessed herself of her corsets before going in to bathe were more subdued. The impulse to weep with helpless mirth whenever she appeared was still there, human nature being what it was; but the story of the Casino episode had flown around the town and cast a damp sheet over the pristine hilarity of the jest. There was the sight of Maurice Walmar's bruised and swollen mouth for reinforcement; and the other aspiring wits looked at it and at the Saint's leathery torso, and merged themselves thoughtfully into the background. Even the waiters, who had been encouraged to curry favour with the sportive element by smirking and winking at the audience whenever they were called upon to serve the woman, relapsed into the supercilious impersonality with which waiters in fashionable resorts cloak their yearnings for tumbrils and guillotines.

Myra Campion cornered the Saint the very next afternoon. He was paddling contentedly along in the general direction of Gibraltar, feeling himself safely insulated from the seethe of popular speculation by the half-mile of limpid water that separated him from the shore, when his head encountered a firm but yielding obstruction. He rolled over and looked into the wet face of Miss Campion.

'You'll have to swim farther out than this if you want to dodge me,' she said.

Destiny having overtaken him, Simon reflected philosophically that it could have chosen many less agreeable vehicles.

'Darling,' he said blandly, 'I've been searching the whole ocean for you.'

She trod water, the slow swell lifting her small brown face against the intense sky, her eyes fixed on him inexorably.

'What was the idea – lashing out at Maurice like that?'

'Did you see what he did?'

'I heard about it. But you didn't have to paste him that way.'

'I just slapped him,' said the Saint calmly. 'Isn't he on the beach today? Well, if I'd really pasted him he'd 've spent the next six weeks in a hospital – getting his face re-modelled.' The Saint steered himself neatly around a drifting jellyfish seeking for its mate. 'My dear, if you're really upset about my slapping a conceited daffodil like Walmar for carrying a joke to those lengths, you haven't the good taste I thought you had.'

There was a certain chilliness about their parting that the Saint realized was unavoidable. He swam back alone, floating leisurely through the buoyant sea and meditating as he went. He knew well enough that a set of diamonds like those displayed by Mrs Porphyria Nussberg are rarely obtained without some kind of inconvenience; but those incidental troubles were merely a part of the most enchanting game in the world.

Back on the sands, he stretched himself out beside Mrs Nussberg's chair and chatted with no more than ordinary politeness. On the following morning he did the same thing. There was no hint of a pressing advance about it; it was simply the way in which any normal holiday acquaintance would have been expected to behave: but the Spanish Cow's soured belligerence had lost its sting. Sometimes she looked at him curiously, with the habitual suspicion hesitating in the background of her beady eyes, as if the impact of a more common courtesy was still too strange to be taken at its face value.

That evening he walked with her along the beach. It was well into cocktail time, and the young brown bodies had taken themselves off the sands to refresh themselves at the Casino or the Perroquet, or to dance before dinner at Maxim's. The last survivor was a shabby mahogany-tanned old man with a rake, engaged in his daily task of scratching the harvest of cigarette-ends and scraps of paper and orange-peel out of the sand to leave it smooth and clean for the morrow's sacrifice – a sad and apocryphal figure on the deserted shore.

They went by the almost empty Fregate; and Simon recalled the caricature in the entrance. It was still there – a brutal, sadistically accurate burlesque. Mrs Nussberg stared fixedly ahead, as if she had forgotten it; but he knew that she had not.

The Saint stepped aside. A lounging waiter realized what was happening too late, and started forward with an outraged yap; but the picture was out of the frame and shredded into small fragments by that time.

Simon held them out on his open hand.

'Do these belong to you?' he inquired gently; and the man suddenly looked up and found the Saint's blue eyes fastened levelly upon him, as hard and wintry as frosted sapphires. The eyes were quite calm, utterly devoid of open menace; but there was something in them that choked his instinctive retort in his throat. Something in the eyes, and the tuned softness of the voice that spoke past them.

He shook his head mutely, astounded at his own silence;

and the Saint smiled genially and dropped the torn relics at his feet.

On the front of the Casino there were banners and posters proclaiming the regular weekly gala.

'Are you going?' asked Simon casually.

The bright defensive eyes switched to him sidelong.

'Are you?'

'I hadn't thought about it.'

They walked a few steps, and then she said sharply: 'Would you come with me?'

Simon did not hesitate for an instant.

'I'd love to,' he said easily; and she said nothing more until he left her at the Provençal.

Before climbing into white shirt and tuxedo, the Saint packed a bag. He was travelling very light; but he still preferred not to leave his preparations for a getaway to the last minute. And he had decided that the getaway should take place that night. He did not want to delay it any longer. He was a little tired of Juan-les-Pins; and, even in that brief time, more than a little tired of the part he had to play.

But when he collected Mrs Nussberg again there was no hint of that in his manner. Her dyed hair had been freshly waved into desperate undulations, and the powder was crusted thickly on her face and arms. Her hands and neck were a blaze of precious stones.

He saw her hard, painted lips smile for the first time.

'You are very kind,' she said as they walked down to the Casino.

The Saint shook his head.

'This gala business is a wonderful racket,' he murmured lightly. 'The same place, the same food, the same music, the same floor show – but they charge you double and let out a few coloured balloons, and everyone thinks they're having a swell time.'

As a matter of strict fact it went a little farther than coloured balloons – Simon, who had attended these events before, had expected it and balanced the factor into his plans. There were rag dolls, for instance – those long-legged sophisticated puppets with which some women love to clutter up their most comfortable chairs. Simon was also able to add a large bouquet of flowers, an enormous box of chocolates, and three of the aforesaid coloured balloons to the bag. When at last he escorted a supremely contented Mrs Nussberg home, he looked rather like an amateur Santa Claus.

Therefore he had a sound excuse for going into the hotel with her; and when she asked for her key at the desk he deftly added that also to his burden.

'You don't want to lug all this stuff upstairs,' he said. 'Let me take them for you.'

She was studying his face again, with that watchful half-suspicious wonderment, as they rode up in the elevator. The elevator boy thought his own cynical thoughts; and under cover of the trophies with which he was laden the Saint pressed Mrs Nussberg's key carefully into a plaque of soft wax, and wrapped the wax delicately in his handkerchief before he put it away.

He went just inside the sitting-room of her suite and decanted the souvenirs on a side table.

'Won't you have a drink?' she asked.

'Thanks,' said the Saint, 'but I think it's past my bedtime.'

She must have been pretty once, it occurred to him as she put down her bag with unaccustomed hesitancy. Pretty in a flashy, common way that had turned only too easily into the obese overblown frowsiness that amused Walmar and his satellites so much.

She held out her hand.

'Thank you so much,' she said with a queer simplicity that had to struggle through the brassy roughness of her voice.

He went back to his own hotel with the memory of that parting in his mind.

She was the Spanish Cow. So he had christened her, and so she would always be. A fat, repulsive, noisy, quarrelsome, imbecile vulgarian – with a two-hundred-thousand-dollar collection of jewels. And it was part of his career to take those jewels away and apply them to a better use than encircling her billowy neck. To make that possible he had to play her like a fish on a line; and it had so happened that the fish had taken the line for a lifeline. It had ceased fighting – had brought itself to a wild, grotesque travesty of coyness. When it discovered how it had been hoodwinked it would fight again – but with other anglers. It would be bitter, coarse, obstreperous again, pulling faces and putting out its tongue. And that also was in the game.

In his room he took a small case of instruments from a drawer and selected a key blank that matched the impression on his wax plaque. It took him a full hour and a half to file a duplicate to his rigorous satisfaction; and then he changed his clothes and picked up an ordinary crook-handle walking-stick and went out again.

It was late enough for him to have the road to himself, and no inquisitive eye observed the course he steered for the fire escape of the Provençal. With the calm dexterity of a seasoned Londoner boarding a passing bus, he edged the crook of his stick over the lowest platform and swung himself nimbly up. Then he flitted up the iron zigzag like a ghost on rubber-soled shoes. The lights were on behind the curtains of a room on the second floor, and a passionate declaration of eternal love wafted out into the balmy night as he went by. The Saint grinned faintly to himself and ascended to the third floor. The nearest window there was dark. He slid over the sill with no more noise than a ray of moonlight, and crossed as silently to the door. In another moment he was outside, the latch jammed back with a wedge of cardboard so that he could make his retreat by the same route, and the corridor stretching out before him like a broad highway to his Eldorado.

The key he had made fitted soundlessly into the lock of Mrs Nussberg's suite, and he turned it without a scrape or a click and let himself into the sitting-room. He had closed the door again from the inside before he saw a thin strip of luminance splitting the darkness on his right, where the communicating door of the bedroom was; and he realized, with a sudden settling of all his faculties into a taut-strung vigilance, that for some unaccountable reason the Spanish Cow had not yet sought the byre.

The Saint rested where he was while he considered the diverse aspects of the misfortune. And then, with the effortless silence of a cat, he glided on towards the bedroom door.

It was at that moment that he heard the incredible noise.

4

For a couple of seconds he thought that after all he must have
been mistaken – that Mrs Nussberg had gone to sleep, leaving the light on as a protection against banshees and things
that go *bomp* in the night, and was snoring with all the high
bulge-like power of which her metallic nasal cavities should
have been capable. Then, as the cadence dropped and he
made out a half-dozen words, he considered whether she
might be giving tongue in her sleep. And then, as the sound
continued, the truth dawned upon him with an eerie shock.

Porphyria Nussberg was singing.

Simon tiptoed to the crack through which the light came.
If there had been lions in the way he could not have stopped
himself. More words came out to him, and the semblance of
a melody that twisted the first tentacles of a slow and awful
understanding into his brain.

She was sitting on the stool in front of her dressing-table,
gazing into the mirror, with her hands spread out inertly
before her. The song was one of those things that the band
had played that night – a song like all the others, a sentimen-
tal dirge to a flimsy tune, with a rhythm that was good to
dance to and a refrain that was true enough for the theme
song of a summer night's illusion. But to Mrs Nussberg it
might have been the Song of Songs. And a weird cold breath
fanned the Saint's spine as it came to him that perhaps it was.

She was singing it with a terrible quiet passion, gazing at
the reflected image of her own face as if in the singing she

saw herself again as she had been when a man desired her. She sang it as if it carried her back to the young years, when it had not been so strange for a handsome cavalier to dance with her without a fee, before time mocked those things into the unthinkable depths of loneliness. Her jewels were heaped in a reluctant pile in front of her. For the first time Simon began to understand them, and he felt that he knew why other women wore them at her age. 'I once was beautiful,' they spoke for her in their pitiful proud defiance. 'I once was young and desired. These stones were given to me because I was beautiful, and a man loved me. Here is your proof.' But she could not have seen them while she sang. She could not have seen anything but the warm, clear flesh on which that creased and painted mask of a face had built itself in the working out of life, to be jeered at and caricatured. She could not have seen anything but the years that go by and leave nothing behind but remembrance. She sang in that cracked, tuneless voice because that night the remembrance had come back – because for a day and a night a man had been kind. And there were tears in her eyes.

The Saint smoked his cigarette. And in a little while he went quietly away, as he had come, and walked home empty-handed under the stars.

Rome
The Latin Touch

I

The city of Rome, according to legend, is built upon the spot where the twin sons of Mars, Romulus and Remus (by a Vestal who must have been somewhat less than virgin), were suckled by a maternally-minded she-wolf; and there were bitter men in the police departments of many countries who would have said that that made it a very appropriate city for Simon Templar to gravitate into, even today. But they would have been thinking of him as a wolf in terms of his predatory reputation rather than in the more innocuous modern connotation of an eye for a pretty girl. He had both, it is true; but it was as a lone wolf in the waste lands of crime that his rather sensational publicity had most featured him.

Simon Templar himself would have said, with an impish twinkle, that this affinity for Rome would be better attributed to the traditional association of the place as a holy city; for who could more aptly visit there than one who was best known by the nickname of 'The Saint'? It troubled him not at all that the incongruity of that sobriquet was a perpetual irritant to the officers of the law who from time to time had been called upon to try and cope with his forays: to revert to the wolf simile, it was enough for him that even his worst enemies had to concede that the sheep who had felt his fangs had always been black sheep.

But that morning, as he stood on the entirely modern pavement outside the ancient Colosseum, his interests were only those of the most ordinary sightseer, and any vulpine instincts he may have had were of the entirely modern kind just referred to – the kind which produces formalized whistles at the sight of a modern Vestal, virtuous or not.

The Saint was too well mannered for such crude compliments, but the girl he was watching could have been no stranger to them. From the top of her close-cropped curly golden head, down through her slim shapely figure and long, slender legs to her thoroughbred ankles, she was fresh, clean, young America incarnate, the new type of goddess that can swim and ride and play tennis and laugh like a boy, to the horror of the conservatives on old Olympus.

Also, as happens all too seldom in real life, she was most providentially in trouble. Providentially from the point of view of any healthy footloose cavalier, that is. She was engaged in a losing argument with the driver of the carriage from which she had just alighted, a beetle-browed individual with all the assurance of a jovial brigand.

'But I made the same trip yesterday,' she was protesting indignantly, 'and it was only two hundred lire!'

'One t'ousand lire,' insisted the driver. 'You give-a me one t'ousand lire, please, *signora*. Dat-a da right-a fare.'

It was all the opening that Simon could have asked.

He strolled up beside the girl.

'Where did you take him from?' he asked.

A pair of level grey eyes sized him up and accepted him gratefully.

'From the Excelsior.'

Simon turned to the driver.

'*Scusami,*' he said pleasantly, '*ma lei scherza?* The fare cannot be one thousand lire.'

'*Mille lire,*' said the driver obdurately. 'It is the legal fare.' He waved his whip in the direction of three or four other unemployed *carrozze* parked expectantly in the shade of the Arch of Constantine. 'Ask any other driver,' he suggested boldly.

'I prefer a more impartial witness,' said the Saint with imperturbable good humour.

He reached out for the blanket that was neatly draped over the seat beside the driver, and flipped it back with a slight flourish. It disclosed a conventional taxi meter which would have been in plain sight of the passenger seat if the blanket had not been so carefully arranged to hide it. Simon's pointing finger drew the girl's eyes to the figures on it.

'One hundred and ninety lire,' he said. 'I'd give him exactly that and forget the tip. It may teach him a lesson – although I doubt it.'

The coachman's unblushing expostulations, accompanied by some scandalous reflections on their ancestry and probable relationship, followed them as the Saint drew her tactfully through the arches and out of earshot.

'All the carriages in Rome have meters, just like a taxi,' he explained easily. 'But there isn't one of them that doesn't have a blanket artistically draped over it, so that you'd never think it was there unless you knew about it. The driver can't lose, and with the average tourist he usually wins. It's brought the country almost as many dollars as the Marshall Plan.'

'I'm the original innocent,' she said ruefully. 'This is my first trip abroad. Do you live here? You speak Italian as if you did.'

'No, but I've been around.'

A seedy-looking character wearing the typical emblem of his fraternity, a two-days' growth of beard, sidled up to them.

'You want a guide?' he suggested. 'I tell you all about the Colosseum. This is where they had the circus. Lions and Christians.'

'I know all about it,' said the Saint. 'In a previous incarnation I was Nero's favourite clown. My name was Emmetus Kellius. Everybody used to laugh themselves sick when the lions bit me. So did I. I was smeared all over with hot mustard.

Unfortunately, though, I was colour-blind. One day, just for a laugh, Poppæa changed the mustard in my make-up pot for ketchup. Everyone said I gave the funniest performance of my life. It even killed me. However—'

The would-be guide stared at him disgustedly and went away.

The girl tried to stop giggling.

'Do you really know anything about it?' she asked. 'It makes me wish I'd paid more attention to Latin when I was in school. But I never got much beyond *Omnia Gallia in tres partes divisa est.*'

'"De Gaulle is divided in three parties,"' he translated brightly. 'I wonder if our State Department knows about that.'

She shot him a sudden sharp glance which he did not understand at the time. It made him think that he was over-doing the flippancy, and he didn't want to spoil such a heaven-sent beginning.

He said, gazing across the arena: 'I don't care about know-ing a lot of dull statistics about it. I just try to imagine it as it was before it began to fall apart. Those tiers with nothing but seats like rows of steps, right up to the top. The bleachers, full of excited bloodthirsty people. The arena baking in the same sun that's on it now.'

'It's so much smaller than I thought it would be.'

'It's bigger than it looks. You could put a football field in the middle and have plenty of room to run around.'

'But the bottom – it's all cut up into sort of dungeons.'

'They probably were. Locker-rooms for the gladiators, cells for the Christians, dens for the wild beasts. They must have been roofed over with planks which rotted away long ago, which made the floor of the arena, with a layer of sand on top for easy cleaning. I expect you could hear everything that went on – from underneath. Until your turn was called . . .

I wonder how many people have come up blinking into this same sunlight that we're seeing, and these stones were the last thing they ever saw?'

She shuddered.

'You make it seem much too real.'

But there were no holiday crowds filling the amphitheatre then. Just a handful of wandering tourists, a few self-appointed guides loafing in hope of a generous audience, a few pedlars with trays of mass-produced cameos. Simon Templar was hardly aware of any of them. He was wholly enjoying the company of the refreshingly lovely girl whom a buccaneer's luck had thrown into his life.

That is why he was completely astounded to realize, in the split second of pain and coruscating lights before unconsciousness rolled over him, that someone had come up behind and hit him on the head.

2

He had to repeat the steps of realization, laboriously, as the blackness slowly dissolved again. His first impression was that he had simply passed out, and he thought hazily of sunstroke, but he couldn't believe that a little sun could do that to him. Then, as a focal point in his skull began to assert itself with painful throbbing, that last instant of awareness came back to him in a flash. He struggled up and opened his eyes.

He was not on the ground, but on a wooden bunk that was almost as hard. There was stone around him, but not the mouldering stones of the Colosseum: these were modern blocks, trimly morticed. A door made of iron bars. And the only evidence of sun was a little light that came through a barred window high above his head.

He could not recall exactly when he had last looked at his watch, but it told him that at least two hours must have passed since he was talking to a delightful young blonde whose name he had not even learned. If he needed anything more than the ache in his head to attest the efficacy of the blow he had taken, the measurement was there on the dial.

He felt in his pockets, thinking stupidly of robbery. They were empty. Robbery might have had something to do with it, but it would not account for the stone walls and the bars.

He was in jail.

He dragged himself to his feet, mastering a desire to vomit, and stumbled to the door. Holding on to the bars, he called out: 'Hey! Hello there!'

It reminded him idiotically of an arty play he had once seen.

Ponderous footsteps clumped deliberately along the passage, and a turnkey came in sight. The uniform clinched any lingering doubt about the jail.

'What am I doing here?' Simon demanded in Italian.

The man surveyed him unfeelingly.

'*Aspette*,' he said, and went away again.

Simon sat down on the hard cot and held his head in his hands, fighting to clear the cobwebs out of it.

Presently there were footsteps again, brisker and more numerous. Simon looked up and found the jailer unlocking the door.

It opened to admit a small delegation. First, in a kind of inverted order of precedence, came a burly police sergeant in uniform. After him came a superior officer in plain clothes, who was slight and rather dapper, but just as obvious a police type in European terms. Those two the Saint might have expected, if he had thought about it, no matter why he was where he was. But it was the third man, for whom they made way only after they had apparently satisfied themselves that the Saint's attitude was not violent, who was the stopper.

He was a tall, iron-grey man with a scholarly stoop, most formally dressed in swallow-tail coat and striped trousers, even carrying white gloves and a silk hat; and Simon recognized him at once. Several million other people would have made the same startled recognition, for Mr Hudson Inverest was not exactly an international nonentity.

'Well,' said the Saint somewhat incredulously, 'this is certainly a new high in service. I know the Secretary of State is technically responsible for people who get themselves in trouble abroad, but I didn't expect you to bail me out in person.'

'You know who I am?' Inverest said matter-of-factly.

The Saint smiled.

'I've seen you in enough news pictures, caricatures – and television. Now I remember reading about you being here on an official visit. It's really very thoughtful of you to be around just at this moment.'

The Secretary stared at him grimly over the top of his glasses.

'Mr Templar, what do you know about my daughter?'

Simon Templar's eyebrows rose a little and drew together.

'Your daughter? I didn't even know you had one.'

The uniformed sergeant started a threatening gesture, but the plain-clothes man checked it with an almost imperceptible movement of his hand.

'My daughter Sue,' Inverest said.

'A willowy blonde?' Simon said slowly. 'With short curly hair and grey eyes?'

'You were with her at the Colossum – just before she was kidnapped.'

It all clicked in the Saint's recuperating mind, with a blind and devastating simplicity – even to a reaction of hers which had puzzled him at the time.

'I was talking to a girl like that,' he said. 'I'd just made some silly crack about the State Department, and I noticed she took it in a rather funny way. But I hadn't the faintest idea who she was. And then I got slugged over the head myself. If there were any witnesses they must have seen that.'

'That was seen,' said the plain-clothes man. 'But it did not explain your presence there.'

'I was unable to leave,' said the Saint. 'I was knocked cold, remember? Do you always arrest any innocent bystander who gets hurt at the scene of a crime?'

'When your pockets were searched for identification,' said the plain-clothes man suavely, 'it was found out at once who you are. Therefore you were brought here. I am sure that being arrested is not such a new experience for you.'

Simon turned to the Secretary.

'Mr Inverest, I never saw your daughter before in my life. I didn't have the faintest idea who she was. I just happened to meet her outside the Colosseum. She was having an argument with a cab driver who was trying to overcharge her. I helped her out, and we went into the place together. We went on talking, naturally. And then I was conked on the head. That's all I know.'

'There were two others,' said the superior policeman impartially. 'After they knocked out Mr Templar, they grabbed Miss Inverest and rushed her out to a car which was waiting outside. I think, your Excellency, that if you give us a little time alone with Mr Templar, we may persuade him to tell us who they were and how he arranged to – as you say – put the finger on your daughter.'

Inverest waved him down impatiently.

'Mr Templar is to be released at once.'

'Your Excellency must be joking.'

'I demand it in the name of the Government of the United States. There is no reasonable charge that can be brought against him.'

'But a man of his reputation—'

Inverest's level grey eyes, oddly reminiscent of his daughter's, searched the Saint's face over his spectacle rims with the same detached appraisal that the girl had given it.

'Inspector Buono,' he said, 'Mr Templar is rumoured to have considerable disregard for the law, but there are no actual charges of law-breaking pending against him in any country. His notoriety, as I understand it, comes from his reprehensible habit of taking the law into his own hands. But it is well known that he is a relentless enemy of criminals. I cannot think of anyone who would be less likely to have any part of such a crime as this. *O si sic omnes!*'

It was a quaintly professorial and almost pedantic speech,

even to the Latin quotation at the end, of the type that frequently made Mr Inverest an easy butt for the more ribald type of political heckling, but his handling of it gave it an austere dignity.

Inspector Buono shrugged helplessly.

They went into an office. The Saint's personal belongings were returned, and a paper was drawn up.

'Your Excellency will have to sign this,' Buono said, with ill-concealed disapproval. 'I have to protect myself. And I hope your Excellency knows what he is doing.'

'I accept full responsibility,' Inverest said, taking out his pen.

Simon watched the signature with the feeling of being at an international conference.

'You're really a big man, sir,' he said, with a sincere respect which came strangely from him. 'Not many people would be capable of giving a ready-made devil like me his due, in a situation like this. Certainly not the average small-time cop.'

Buono scowled.

'*Damnant quod non intelligunt*,' Inverest said wryly. 'It's part of my job to be some sort of judge of human nature. Besides, I have access to special information. I checked on your record in Washington while we were waiting for you to come to. I talked to the man who was in charge of the O.S.S. section you worked for during the last war.'

'Hamilton?'

'He gave you quite a remarkable reference.'

Simon lighted a cigarette. He had almost forgotten the throbbing in his head, and his brain was starting to feel normal again.

'I wish I could be some use to you now,' he said sympathetically. 'I liked your daughter a lot . . . If I'd only had the least idea who she was, I might have been a little on guard. But there wasn't any reason for me to be suspicious of anyone who came near us. How come she was running around on her own like that, without any kind of protection? Or does that question embarrass Inspector Buono?'

'A special escort was provided for Miss Inverest,' Buono said coldly. 'But she gave them the slip. Deliberately, I am told.'

'There was a young fellow detailed by the Embassy to take her around, too,' Inverest said, 'and she stood him up. Sue's always been like that. She hates the V.I.P. treatment. Getting away from Secret Service men and all that sort of thing is just like playing hookey from school to her. She says she just wants to get around on her own and see things like any ordinary girl. I can't really blame her. I couldn't be telling her all the time what special danger she might be in.'

'Do you have some idea what the special danger might be right now?' Simon asked.

'Unfortunately, I do. In fact, I know it.'

Inverest took off his spectacles and rubbed his eyes. That mechanical movement was the first break in his spartan self-control, the first outward betrayal of the desperate anxiety that must have been eating his insides.

'Does the name Mick Unciello mean anything to you?'

'I read all the crime news,' said the Saint, with a slight smile. 'He was the official executioner of the Mid-western crime syndicate. The F.B.I. finally got the goods on him, and he was sentenced to the chair some time ago.'

'His final appeal to the Supreme Court was rejected last week.'

'The Supreme Court can collect a bouquet from me.'

'Now, do you remember the name Tony Unciello?'

'Yes. He was the vice lord in the same syndicate. The F.B.I. didn't do so well with him, but they were able to get him deported – I think that was in 1948.'

'Mick Unciello, of course, is the younger brother of Tony. And Tony is here in Italy.'

'It begins to figure,' said the Saint quietly.

'Nothing can save Mick Unciello's life now except the personal intervention of the President,' Inverest said in his dry, schoolmasterish voice. 'That, of course, is unthinkable. But it may be quite another matter to convince Tony that my influence would not be enough to bring it about.'

'Is this something more than a fast guess on your part?'

'Oh, yes,' said the Secretary wearily. 'I've already had a telephone call from a person claiming to be Tony Unciello, and I have no reason to doubt its authenticity. He said that unless Mick Unciello was reprieved, Sue would die, too – but more slowly.'

Simon Templar drew at his cigarette, holding it with fingers that were almost self-consciously steady. The naturally devil-may-care lines of his strong reckless face might never have known laughter. He faced the set-up in all its naked ugliness. A memory of Sue Inverest's gay, clean-limbed confident youth slid across his mind, and his stomach curled again momentarily.

Then his eyes went to the sleek Inspector.

'But if it's as open as all that,' he said, 'why haven't you picked up Tony Unciello?'

'It is not so easy,' Buono said stonily. 'Unciello has dropped out of sight since several days. You understand, there was nothing against him here, so he is not watched all the time. Now, he cannot be found. We look for him, of course, but it is not a simple matter of going to his apartment. He is hiding.'

'And you haven't any idea where to look.'

'It is not made easy for us.'

'What Inspector Buono isn't saying,' Inverest put in, 'is that the Unciellos are both members of the Mafia. Tony himself is reputed to be one of the very top men. Perhaps you don't know what a stranglehold that terroristic secret society has on this country. Nobody knows how many members there are, but at least three-quarters of the population are scared to death of them. If a man of Unciello's class wants to disappear, there are thousands who would help to hide him, and literally millions who wouldn't betray him if they knew where he was.'

The Saint took another long drag at his cigarette. He tilted his head back and exhaled the smoke in a trickle of seemingly inexhaustible duration, watching it with rapt lazy-lidded blue eyes.

'Just the same,' he said. 'I think I know how to find him.'

3

It was as if he had hit them with a paralysis ray out of some science-fiction story. Hudson Inverest stiffened where he sat. Inspector Buono made one sharp jerky movement and then froze.

'Do you mean you know more about this than you've told us?' Inverest said.

Simon nodded.

'Funny things happen when you're knocked out,' he said. 'I was hit on the head, and I went down like a wet rag. But I didn't black out all at once. My eyes must have gone on working for several seconds, like a camera with a shutter left open, before I passed out completely. And then, when I first recovered consciousness, I'd forgotten all about what I saw. Now it's suddenly all come back – as if the film had been developed. I know I can find Tony Unciello.'

'What did you see?' Buono demanded.

Simon looked him in the eyes.

'I can't tell you.'

'I do not understand you, *signor!*'

'What I saw happens to be something that wouldn't be any use at all to anyone else. I'm the only man in the world who could use it. So I shall keep it to myself – until I've found Tony. I don't think it'll take very long.'

'That is absurd!' Buono insisted waspily. 'I insist that you tell us how you propose to do this.'

The Saint turned to Inverest.

'I will tell you, sir, in private, and let you be the judge. But I'm quite sure you'll agree with me. You see, what I know has some really shocking political complications. If it leaked out, the international repercussions would be bigger than an atom bomb. If you knew what I know, you'd be the first to order me to keep my mouth shut.'

Inspector Buono bounced to his feet.

'It is against the law to conceal information about a crime from the police,' he said furiously. 'This alters everything. I shall refuse to release you!'

Inverest gazed at the Saint intently from under lowered brows.

'He has already been released,' he pointed out at length. 'Furthermore, as regards anything that has transpired since then, I must inform you that Mr Templar has just been appointed a special attaché to the American Embassy, and therefore claims diplomatic immunity.' He stood up. 'I shall communicate with you later, Inspector, if I decide that Mr Templar's information should be disclosed. Come, Mr Templar.'

He gestured with his shiny top hat towards the door, and Simon went and opened it.

The Secretary of State stalked out without a backward glance, but Simon Templar could not resist turning to give the baffled Inspector a mocking bow before he followed.

Uniformed guards outside saluted them into a waiting black limousine with CD plates and the Stars and Stripes fluttering from a little mast on the hood. It was the finest exit the Saint had ever made from any police station, and he would treasure the remembrance for the rest of his life – however long that might be.

'The driver is an Italian,' Inverest said. 'Better wait until we're alone.'

Simon nodded, and said nothing more until the door had

closed behind them in the office at the Embassy which had been placed at the Secretary's disposal.

'Well, Mr Templar,' Inverest said, dropping his hat and gloves on the desk, 'you've placed me in a most peculiar position. Unless you have something extraordinary up your sleeve, I might well deserve to be impeached. All that talk of yours about international complications, of course, was arrant nonsense.'

'You realized that, did you?'

'I'm not completely naïve.'

'After what you said about the Mafia,' Simon explained, 'I couldn't take any chances. Not even in police headquarters. It'd only take one tiny leak to blow the whole works. And that'd mean good-bye to Sue.'

'That's understood,' Inverest said brusquely. 'I took the risk of backing you up. But what is it that you know?'

Simon took out a cigarette and placed it between his lips. Then he took out his lighter and held it poised.

'Nothing.'

He lighted the cigarette.

Hudson Inverest's features seemed to crumple from inside, as if he had received a physical blow. He sank slowly into a chair.

'Good God, man,' he cried shakily. 'What are you saying?'

'I don't know a thing. I haven't a clue. I was knocked cold on the spot, and that was the end of it. But,' Simon went on quickly, 'nobody knows that except you and me.'

Inverest clasped his hands together as if to steady them.

'Go on.'

'If there's a leak in the police department,' said the Saint, 'so much the better. It'll make the story that much more convincing when it gets to Tony. But we're not going to gamble on that chance alone. I want you to call in your public relations boys and tell them to see that every newspaper in

Rome gets the story. Let 'em be as mysterious as they like, but sell it big. Then we'll know for sure that Tony Unciello will hear it. His men already know that they slugged a guy who was with Sue, but they didn't know who it was. My name'll hit them with a big bang. I think it'll make 'em believe almost anything.'

'But if they do believe it,' Inverest said, 'what good will it do? They'll just shoot you down in the street.'

Simon shrugged.

'That's quite a possibility. But I'm betting on the angle of curiosity. I don't think a man like Unciello could bear never to know what this one thing was that I had on him. So I think he'll want me taken alive.'

'Even so,' Inverest protested, 'if they catch you and take you to him – what would you be able to do?'

'I'll try to think of that when the time comes.' Simon stood over the older man, very lean and straight, and something like the strength of a sword invested him. 'But it's the only chance we've got of finding your daughter. You've got to let me try it.'

The statesman blinked up at him, trying to dispel a ridiculous illusion that a musketeer's feather tossed above that impossibly handsome face.

'It might still cost you your life,' he said.

'For a gal like Sue,' said the Saint lightly, 'I wouldn't call that expensive.'

4

Simon Templar came out of the front gates of the Embassy and stood on the pavement for a while gazing idly up and down the Via Vittorio Veneto, like a man trying to make up his mind where to go. What he wanted was to be sure that anyone who might already be watching for him outside would not be left flat-footed by too sudden a departure.

Presently he walked a few steps to the entrance of the Hotel Excelsior, which was only next door. He paused inside to give the lobby a leisurely survey, and at the same time to give the population of the lobby plenty of time to survey him. Then he crossed to the porter's desk.

'Do you have any messages for me?' He added, very clearly: 'The name is Templar – Simon Templar.'

'Your room number, sir?'

'Six-seventeen.'

The porter examined his pigeon-holes.

'No, Mr Templar.'

'Thank you. Where is the cocktail bar?'

'On the left, sir, down the stairs.'

That ought to take care of anyone who might be waiting to pick him up at the hotel.

He went down the stairs. The room was filling up, the hour being what it was, but he found a place at the bar and ordered a Dry Sack. He was aware of other people filtering in after him – at least two couples, and a single man who sat at the far end of the bar and started reading a newspaper. But Simon paid none of them any direct attention. He watched more carefully to see the bottle taken off the shelf and his drink poured without any legerdemain. After all, he reflected, the Borgias were Italians, and any bartender would be a likely candidate for the Mafia.

The general level of conversation, he was pleased to note, was pitched discreetly low.

He said to the bartender, just loudly enough for anyone who cared to overhear: 'Tell me, I hear there are two restaurants claiming to be the original Alfredo's – the place that's famous for *fettucini*. Which is the real one?'

The bartender grinned.

'Ah, yes, they make such propaganda against each other. But the real one, the old one, is in the Viadella Scrofa.'

'Then I must have been taken to the imitation last night. Tonight I'll have to try the old original.'

'You will have a good dinner.'

And that should be plenty of help to anyone who picked up the trail late, or who wanted to make plans ahead . . .

But nothing was likely to happen in the Excelsior cocktail lounge, which was obviously not adapted to tidy abductions, and the Saint was too impatient to wait there for long. The laughing face of Sue Inverest kept materializing in front of him, turning into a mask of pitiful terror, dissolving into imagined scenes of unspeakable vileness. He knew the mentality of men like Tony Unciello too well to be complacent about the inevitable passing of time. He wanted something to happen fast. He wanted to leave nothing undone that would help it to happen.

He finished his sherry, paid for it, and went out into the street again.

A glance at his watch only reasserted the fact that it was still early to go to dinner. He strolled up towards the Borghese Park, making a conscious effort to slow down a stride that wanted to hurry but had no place to hurry to.

The crowded tables of a pavement café were suddenly on both sides of him. Perhaps there, Unciello's men might see an opportunity.

He saw a vacant table at the edge of the pavement, next to the street, where it would be as easy as possible for them, and sat down.

A waiter took his order. A boy came by with an armful of newspapers, and Simon bought one. The kidnapping of Sue Inverest qualified for the biggest headline on the front page, and early in the story he found himself referred to as a friend of the girl, who had been 'beaten and left for dead' on the scene; with a fine disregard for obvious probabilities, which was no more inconsistent than the facts, he was later reported being held by the police for investigation of his possible complicity in the crime.

His drink came, and he paid for it but did not touch it. He extracted a grim kind of satisfaction out of realizing that the chances of any food or drink offered to him being poisoned must be increasing with every minute. He could cope with that danger easily enough, at least for a while. It was less easy to become accustomed to the crawly feeling that at any instant a knife from nowhere might strike him between the shoulder-blades, or a fusillade of shots from a passing car smash him down into bloody oblivion. But that was what he had asked for; and he was beginning to sympathize with the emotions of a goat that had not merely been staked out to attract a tiger, but was co-operating with every resource of capric coquetry to coax the tiger to the bait. And all he could do was hope he was not mistaken in his estimate of Tony Unciello's vein of curiosity . . .

He read on, looking for a reference to the mysterious secret clue he was supposed to have.

And then he had company.

There were two of them, and because he had studiously

avoided watching for them they might have sprung up out of the ground. They stood one on each side of him, crowding him, and at the same time practically blocking him from the sight of the other patrons of the café. They were men of perfectly average size and build, dressed in perfectly common-place dark suits, with perfectly unmemorable faces distinguished only by the perfect expressionlessness of their prototypes in any gangster movie. It was just like home.

The street was behind Simon; but that opening was closed, with admirable timing, by a car which simultaneously slid into the kerb and stopped at his back.

One of the men leaned on Simon's shoulder with a hand that was buried in his coat pocket, but what the Saint felt was harder than a hand, and he knew that the muzzle of a gun was no more than an inch from his car.

'Let's-a go, sport,' the man said.

Simon tried to look up with the right combination of fear, surprise and bluster.

'What are you talking about?'

'You, sport,' said the spokesman laconically. 'Get in-a da car.'

Simon flicked his cigarette into the gutter, where it was immediately the centre of a scramble of vulture-eyed urchins, and stood up. It was the only stir caused by his departure.

In the car, the two men sat one on each side of him in the back seat. Each of them kept a hand in the pocket of his coat on the side nearest the Saint, one in the right, one in the left. Their two guns pressed with equal firmness against the neighbourhood of the Saint's kidneys. Neither of them offered any conversation. The driver of the car said nothing. He drove in competent silence, like a man who already had his instructions.

There were no shades inside the car, no suggestion of blindfolding the Saint, no attempt to stop him observing the route they took. The implication that nothing he saw would ever be any use to him was too obvious to be missed, but that gave him nothing unforeseen to worry about. He could still hope that the project was to take him to Tony Unciello before the only possible intended end of the ride.

They drove down to the Tiber, crossed over the Ponte Cavour, turned by the Palace of Justice. The great white dome of St Peter's loomed ahead against the darkening sky, and lights played on the fountains in the vast circular piazza in front of the cathedral, but they left it on their right and skimmed around the walls of the Vatican City to plunge into the maze of mean streets which lies incongruously between it and the pleasant park slopes of Monte Gianicolo. A few zigzags through narrow, ill-lit alleys, and the car stopped outside a small *pizzeria* and bar with strings of salami tastefully displayed in the dingy window.

'Get out, sport,' said the talking man.

His partner got out first and waited for the Saint. The two of them closed in behind Simon and prodded him towards the door of the *pizzeria*. They kept him moving briskly through the odorous interior, but it was only to get their job done, not because they cared about anyone in the place. The drinkers at the bar just inside the entrance, the shirt-sleeved bartender wiping glasses on a filthy rag, the few diners at the stained tables in the back, the slatternly woman who looked out of the open door of the kitchen in the rear, all stared at the Saint silently as he passed; but the stares were as emotionless and impersonal as the stares of zombies.

Next to the kitchen door there was a curtained archway; beyond it, a steep flight of stairs. They climbed to a narrow landing with two doors. The man who never spoke opened one of them and pushed the Saint through.

He found himself in a small, untidy bedroom, but he hardly had time to glance over it before the same man was doing something to the big old-fashioned wardrobe which caused it to roll noiselessly aside like a huge sliding door.

'Kepp-a moving, sport,' said the talkative one, and the Saint was shoved on through the opening.

As he stepped into the brightness beyond, as if on to a stage set, he knew that he had at least won the first leg of the double, even before he saw the man who waited for him.

'Hullo, Tony,' he said.

5

It was the contrast of the room in which he found himself after the squalor that he had been hustled through which was theatrical. It was spacious and high-ceilinged, exquisitely decorated and furnished, like a room in a set designer's conception of a ducal palace. The Saint's gaze travelled leisurely around it in frank fascination. From his impression of the street outside he realized that the interiors of several ramshackle old buildings must have been torn out to provide a shell for that luxurious hideaway – a project that only a vast secret society could have undertaken and kept secret. Even the absence of windows was almost unnoticeable, for the indirect lighting was beautifully engineered and the air was fresh and cool.

'Quite a layout you have, for such a modest address,' Simon remarked approvingly. 'And with air-conditioning, yet.'

'Sure, it's plenty comfortable,' said Tony Unciello.

He sat in an immense brocaded chair, looking like a great gross frog. The resemblance held true for his sloping hairless head, his swarthy skin and heavy-lidded reptilian eyes, his broad stomach and thin splayed legs. In fact, almost the only un-froglike things about him were his clothes, the diamond rings on his fingers, and the cigar clamped in his wide, thick-lipped mouth.

'So you're the Saint,' Unciello said. 'Sit down.'

Instantly Simon was pushed forward, the seat of an upright chair hit him behind the knees, and two hands on his shoulders pushed him forcefully down on it. His two escorts stood behind him like sentries.

The Saint straightened his coat.

'Really, Tony,' he murmured, 'when you get hospitable, it's just like being caught in a reaper.'

The gangster took the cigar out of one side of his mouth and put it back in the other.

'I heard a lot about you, Saint.'

'I know. And you just couldn't wait to meet me.'

'I could of waited for ever to meet you. But now it's different. All on account of this place.' Unciello took the cigar out again to wave it comprehensively at the surroundings. 'It's quite a layout, like you said. And comfortable, like I said. You ain't seen a half of it. I could hole up here for years, and live just like the Ritz. Only there's nobody supposed to know about it who don't belong to me, body and soul. And then you come along, and you don't belong to me, but it gives out that you know how to find me.'

'Why, what gave you that idea?'

'That's what you said.'

'I'd bought a newspaper just before your reception committee picked me up,' Simon remarked thoughtfully, 'but it didn't have that story. How did you hear it so quickly? Direct from the police, maybe?'

'You catch on fast,' Unciello said. 'Sure, Inspector Buono's one of my boys. He should of kept you locked up when he had you, and saved me this trouble.'

Simon nodded. He was not greatly surprised.

'I figured him for a bad egg,' he said. 'But it's nice to have you confirm it.'

'Buono's a good boy,' Unciello said. 'He knows where I am. That's okay. But with you it's different.' He leaned forward a little. His manner was very patient and earnest. 'I like this place. Spent a lot of dough fixing it up. I'd hate that it be all wasted. But when a fellow like you says he could find it, it bothers me. I gotta know how you got it figured. So if maybe somebody slipped up somewhere, it can be taken care of. See what I mean?'

'You couldn't be more lucid, Tony,' Simon reassured him. 'And what do you think this information would be worth?'

Unciello chuckled, a soundless quaking of his wide belly.

'Why, to you it's worth plenty. You tell me all about it, and everything's nice and friendly. But you don't tell me, and the boys have to go to work on you. They do a mean job. You hold out for an hour, a day, two days – depending how tough you are. But in the end you talk just the same, only you been hurt plenty first. To a fellow with your brains that don't make sense. So you tell me now, and we don't have no nastiness.'

Simon appeared to consider this briefly, but the conclusion was obvious.

'You make everything delightfully simple,' he said. 'So I'll try to do the same. I said I could find you, and this proves it. I'm here now.'

'Only because my boys brought you here.'

'Which I figured you'd have them do as soon as you heard I was claiming to know how to find you.'

Unciello's eyes did not blink so much as deliberately close and open again, like the eyes of a lizard.

'You're a smart fellow. Now you're here. What's your angle?'

'Will one of these goons behind me start shooting if I go for a cigarette?'

'Not if it's just a cigarette.'

Simon took one from the pack in his breast pocket, moving slowly and carefully to avoid causing any alarm. In the same way he took out his lighter and kindled it.

'I'm acting as Mr Inverest's strictly unofficial representative,' he said. 'As you very well know, he can't officially make

any deal with you. In fact, for public consumption he's got to
say loudly that nobody can blackmail him, even with his
daughter's life – or else he'd probably be out of a job and
have no influence at all. But as a man, of course, you've got
him over a barrel. He's ready to trade.'

'He's a smart fellow, too.'

'It'll have to be very discreetly handled, so that it looks
kosher. They'll have to arrange to dig up some startling new
evidence, to give grounds for a re-trial and an acquittal.'

'That's his worry. I don't care how he does it, just so Mick
gets out.'

'But before he starts to work he's got to be sure that you've
really got his daughter and that she hasn't been harmed.'

'The gal's okay.'

Simon looked at him steadily.

'I have to see her myself. Then I'll write him a note,
which you can have delivered. I'll tell you right now that
it'll have a code word in it, which is to prove that I really
wrote it and that nobody was twisting my arm to make me
say the right things.'

Unciello contemplated him with the immobility of a
Buddha. Then his eyes switched to a point over the Saint's
head.

'*Mena la giovane*,' he said.

The hoodlum who never spoke came around from behind
the Saint's chair and crossed the big room to disappear
through one of the doors at the other end. Unciello smoked
his cigar impassively. There was no idle conversation.
Presently the man who had left came back, and with him he
brought Sue Inverest.

She was so exactly like Simon had seen her last, and as he
remembered her, that for a moment it felt as if they were
back in the Colosseum. Only in a strange dislocation of time
they now seemed to belong rather with the expendables who

had once stood on the floor of the arena, while a modern but no less vicious Nero squatted like a toad on his brocaded throne and held their lives in his hands. But the girl still carried her curly fair head high, and Simon smiled into her shocked grey eyes.

'Your father sent me to see if you were all right, Sue,' he said gently. 'Have they hurt you?'

'No, not yet. Are they going to let me go?'

'Quite soon, I hope.'

'Write that letter,' Unciello said.

The taciturn thug brought a pad and pencil from a side table and thrust them at the Saint.

Simon balanced the pad on his knee and wrote, taking his time:

> *Dear Mr Inverest,*
> *I've seen Sue, and she's as good as new. So you'd better hurry up and meet Tony's terms, even if it isn't exactly 'for the public good'. Perhaps that would sound better to you in Latin, but it all comes to the* homo sequendum. *Will report again as arranged.*
>
> > *Simon Templar.*

He held out the pad. The man who had brought it carried it across to Unciello.

Unciello read it through slowly, and looked up again at the Saint.

'What's that *homo sequendum* deal?' he demanded.

'*Homo* means "same", as in "*homosexual*",' Simon explained patiently. '*Sequendum* is the same root as our words "sequel" or "*consequences*". It just means "the same result". Inverest goes for that Latin stuff.'

Unciello's eyes swivelled up the the girl.

'That's right,' she said in a low voice. 'He does.'

'Guys like you with your education give me a pain,' Unciello said. His cold stare was on the Saint again. 'And what's that about reporting again?'

'I'm not stupid enough to expect you to turn me loose now,' Simon said. 'And anyhow, Inverest is going to want another report on Sue — authenticated with our password — from me, before they finally let your brother go.'

The gang chieftain held out the pad towards his errand-boy.

'Have somebody downstairs send it,' he ordered.

He continued to study the Saint emotionlessly, but with deep curiosity.

'You're a real smart fellow,' he said. 'But you're taking a lot of chances. What's in it for you?'

Simon raised his eyebrows a fraction.

'Hudson Inverest is a rich man in his own right,' he said. 'He's offered a reward of a hundred thousand dollars to anyone who helps get his daughter back. Didn't your pal Buono tell you that? Even he looked interested!'

The messenger returned and resumed his position behind the Saint's chair, but Unciello did not even appear to notice him for several seconds. He remained sunk in an implacable and frightening immobility of meditation. And then at last his saurian eyes flicked up.

'Tell Mario to serve dinner,' he said. 'We'll all eat together. And send word to Buono I want to see him — *subito.*'

6

They ate in a palatial dining-room that was almost over-
poweringly ornate with gilt and frescoes, Sue and the Saint
on either side of Tony Unciello at the head of a long table.
One of the guards stood behind each of the involuntary
guests like an attendant footman, but their function was not
to serve. They kept their hands in the side pockets of their
coats and their eyes on every movement that was made,
particularly by the Saint.

The meal, in spite of the lavish surroundings, was only
spaghetti, though with an excellent sauce. Apparently that
was what Unciello liked, for he tackled a huge plate of it with
a practically uninterrupted series of engulfing motions,
almost inhaling it in a continuous stream. Sue Inverest could
only toy with hers, but the Saint ate with reasonable appetite,
although the grotesque silence broken only by the clink of
silverware and the voracious slurping of the host would have
unnerved most other men.

'Tony doesn't like small talk at meals,' Simon tried to
encourage her, 'but don't let him put you off your feed.
You've got to keep in good shape to go home.'

Unciello stuffed the last remnants from his plate into his
mouth until his cheeks bulged, then washed them down with
a draught of Chianti from a Venetian goblet. He wiped his
face with the napkin tucked under his chin.

'Now I got it,' he announced; and the Saint looked at him
inquiringly.

Unciello said: 'I get that *homo sequendum* business. That's gotta be the password you fixed up with Inverest. It's the only phony-sounding thing in your letter. So now I don't need you any more. I got boys who can copy any handwriting. And with that password, now *they* can write letters to Inverest and tell him his daughter's okay.'

'You mean I can go, Tony?' Simon asked hopefully.

'Yeah – to the morgue. You never was going anywhere else, because you know too much about this place. Like I told you. But now I don't have to keep you around until they let Mick go. I guess you ain't so smart, after all.'

Simon Templar had no argument. It would have done no good to point out that this was one occasion when he had never figured himself very smart, so far as his own personal survival was concerned. He felt lucky enough to have achieved as much as he had done. Now, if he was not going to live to see the finish, he could still hope that the gamble had not been altogether lost. As for himself, it had to come some day, and this was as worth while as any.

He smiled at the girl's comprehending horror, and his eyes were very gay and blue.

'Don't worry, Sue,' he said. 'Don't think about it, ever. I just hope everything works out all right for you.'

'I'll take care of her myself, personally,' Unciello said: and only then, for the first time, Simon felt ice in his heart.

The door from the living-room opened abruptly, and Inspector Buono came in.

He looked very cool and elegant; and if he had any nervousness, it might only have been found in his eyes. They merely glanced at the girl and Simon, and went quickly back to Unciello.

'*Eccomi arrivato*,' he said obsequiously. '*Cosa desidera?*'

'Talk English,' Unciello growled. 'The Saint wants to know what's going on. It's his funeral we're talking about. I sent for you because you're just the boy to take charge of it. You got the perfect set-up. You make it look like he was shot resisting arrest. You do it yourself, and maybe get yourself a medal.'

'But—'

'I'm sending a couple of the boys along to watch you.' Unciello poured another glass of wine, and his broad face was malevolently bland. 'I hear some of our people are worried that one of these days you might get too interested in a reward, if it was big enough. Now, if they see you do something like this, so they can feel they've got something on you, it'll give 'em a lot more confidence.'

'*Sissignor*,' Buono said whitely.

Then the door behind him burst open again, and the room suddenly filled with armed police.

Through their midst stepped a large, elderly, perspiring man with a superb black handle-bar moustache, who surveyed the scene with somewhat pompous satisfaction.

'Everyone here,' he said, not without a trace of awe, 'is under arrest.'

The stooped, scholarly figure of the Secretary of State followed him in, and Sue Inverest flung herself into her father's arms.

Simon Templar prudently reached for the Chianti bottle and refilled his glass.

7

Most of what Sue Inverest did not know had been told her while the official limousine was still on its way to the Embassy.

'But I still don't know how you got there,' she said, 'like – like the posse coming over the hill in the last reel of a western.'

'My dear,' Mr Inverest said mildly, 'surely even you learned enough Latin in school to know that *homo sequendum* means "man who must be followed"?'

She gave a shaky half-laugh.

'I might have thought of that, but the Saint was so convincing with his translation . . . And anyway, how did you know *who* to follow?'

'Whom,' said Mr Inverest.

'You remember that tag about "for the public good"?' Simon said. 'I told your father he'd like it better in Latin. That's *pro bono publico*. I could only hope he'd be fast enough to turn the *bono* into *Buono*.'

'Fortunately I'm not quite the imbecile that I'm sometimes called,' Inverest said. 'Once I had that clue, I went straight to the top. That was the Minister of the Interior himself, who was in charge of the raid.'

'And you remember,' Simon added, 'how I threw in that bit about Buono's unseemly interest in a reward which he hadn't reported – for the simple reason that it was never offered. I was banking on that to bother Tony enough so that he'd send for Buono, which would lead the posse straight to the right place.'

The girl cuddled her father's arm, but her grey eyes were on the Saint.

'I know you're not really rich, Daddy,' she said. 'But he ought to have some reward.'

Simon grinned.

'I'll settle for the privilege of buying you a real dinner. And then maybe dancing with you till dawn. And then if there's anything still owing, I'd better leave it on deposit, I'm liable to need it one of these days,' said the Saint.